Véro and Philippe

Véro and Philippe

Caroline Hatton

Illustrated by Preston McDaniels

Front Street / Cricket Books
Chicago

*With special thanks to Cindy Kolodny's Writers Group,
Collyn Justus, and my editor, John Allen, who provided a
warm haven for me to grow as a writer.*
—C.H.

Text copyright © 2001 by Caroline Hatton
Illustrations copyright © 2001 by Preston McDaniels
Printed in the United States of America
Designed by Anthony Jacobson
First edition, 2001

Library of Congress Cataloging-in-Publication Data

Hatton, Caroline Kim
   Véro and Philippe / Caroline Hatton; illustrated by Preston McDaniels.—1st ed.
      p. cm.
   Summary: When Mother fires the housekeeper, life becomes difficult for the entire Vo
family, Vietnamese immigrants to France in 1964, but nine-year-old Véro and her
twelve-year-old brother, Philippe, work together to try to convince Mother to rehire her.
   ISBN 0-8126-2940-X
   [1. Family life—France—Fiction. 2. Brothers and sisters—Fiction.
3. Vietnamese—France—Fiction. 4. Latchkey children—Fiction. 5. Household
employees—Fiction. 6. Paris (France)—Fiction. 7. France—Fiction.] I. McDaniels,
Preston, ill. II. Title.

   PZ&.H2848 Ve 2001
   [Fic]—dc21

00-047651

A Grand Savant
La Sœur
(To Great Scholar
from The Sister)
—C.H.

To Cindy, for all her love and patience
—P.M.

Contents

My Summer Vacation

I pressed my nose on the window to peer at the cobbled street below. There wasn't a single tree where my father could hang a swing. There would never be another frog for my brother to catch, to make me laugh and make my mother shriek. There was no life, only grownups hurrying to some Terribly Important Meeting.

Back in Normandy, no one hurried.

In Paris, everything was gray: the evening clouds, the stone buildings, the cobblestones, even the pigeons asleep on the window sills. The only thing with any color had been dropped on the sidewalk by a dog.

"It's all your fault we had to move," I said to my brother, Philippe. "Just so you wouldn't have to go to a boarding school."

He was unpacking his prize airplane, the blue one with a propeller powered by a giant rubber band. Making loud engine noises, he landed it on top of his bookcase next to the rest of his gleaming fleet.

"Of course we moved just for me," he said. "I'm a Great Scholar, and Paris is where the best schools are. I'm going to get good grades and learn English and build airplanes with real motors."

"But I *can't* go to school in Paris," I whimpered. "I won't know what to do." My stomach felt like it was in the wrong place, and so did I.

"Don't worry, Véro," said Philippe. "I'll help you get ready. School is the same everywhere. The first day back,

1

the teacher will make you write about your summer vacation."

My heart sank. "What vacation? We didn't do anything except move here. I have nothing to write about. Nothing. I'll get a bad grade." I almost fainted at my own words.

"No you won't," said Philippe. "You just have to write something really exciting, like city kids do. I have an idea."

He opened a box labeled *Philippe's stuff* and took out his favorite comic books: Astérix, the Gaul who always defeated the Roman invaders, and Buck Danny, the American pilot. "Pick one," he said. I pointed at Buck Danny. It was in French, except for a few useful English words like "Mayday." Philippe chose a paragraph at the top of a picture. "Learn this by heart," he said.

"Are you sure?" I squeaked, trembling.

"Absolutely," he said. "I've been in school three years longer than you. I've been through all this before. Trust me."

But, I thought, that was in Normandy. What if teachers were different in Paris? How would he know? My mind went wild. But Philippe made me sit at his big mahogany desk and copy the paragraph over and over again. Little by little, my racing heart slowed down.

Meanwhile, he flopped on his bed to read *Astérix*. He'd read it a million times, yet it was still like new, not like my books.

I said, "I'm getting a cramp in my hand."

"*Sh,*" said Philippe. "Keep writing."

So I did, with a sigh.

I didn't belong in Paris. I belonged in Normandy. That's where I was born, nine years earlier, after my parents had flown halfway around the world to emigrate from Vietnam to France. Together they had run the village pharmacy, the only one for kilometers around. In Normandy, when we drove from forest to horse farm along the red poppy fields, the peasants rested their pitchforks and waved. In Paris no one knew us, and my parents' new pharmacy was lost among hundreds of shops. Here, the streets were lined with tall buildings that all looked the same, like raindrops. How could my parents and my brother be so excited about this move?

My writing exercise ended when my mother marched in to trumpet, "Bedtime!" She escorted me toward my new bedroom, but I stopped to watch my father rest a big box labeled *encyclopedia* on the corner of the telephone table.

"Too heavy," he said in Vietnamese. No surprise— he was so thin. He adjusted his wire glasses atop his important nose.

My mother told him, also in Vietnamese, to carry just a few books at a time. Then she switched back to French as she grabbed my wrist and walked on. "Let's get you tucked into bed. Francine will be here any minute."

"Can't I stay up to play with her?" I asked.

"No," said my mother. "You know I don't allow her to play." She put me in bed carefully, as if she were shelving her Sunday shoes.

"Can she sleep in my room?" I asked.

"Absolutely not. Her room is outside our apartment, on the top floor of the building."

It was hopeless.

"I don't want to go to school tomorrow," I said. "Can I stay home to help unpack?"

My mother plopped her plump self on the edge of my bed and said, "You've helped so much already. I think we can take it from here."

"But I went to school for years in Normandy," I said. "It's time for me to get a job."

"Your job is to go to sleep." She kissed me and turned off the light. I didn't have the heart to say any more.

My father came in. "Sweet dreams," he said. "You'll see Francine at breakfast."

FRANCINE WAS OUR MAID in Normandy. Back there, she used to come and clean our house once a week. She'd also milk the cows on her parents' farm every single day. She was twenty years old.

The summer before, my parents had explained that in Paris, we'd no longer live above the pharmacy. My mother wouldn't be able to do chores between clients, so they'd asked Francine to come with us and do housework and watch us children in exchange for a room, three meals a day, and a little pay. She'd dropped her milk pails and jumped at the chance to move to the city.

IN THE MORNING, Francine was in the kitchen, humming and stirring chocolate powder into my bowl of hot milk. I wasn't hungry, but my mother made me eat breakfast anyway, bread with butter and jam. Afterward, she helped me get dressed. I picked my bluest school smock. Then she dragged me out the apartment door, down the stairs, out of the building, and down the street to school. Francine came along to learn her way around.

"Beginning tomorrow, Francine will walk you to and from school," my mother said.

In Normandy, our street was the whole village. Beyond it was lush green country, shimmering with wildflowers, alive with birdsong, whinnies, and moos. Here, all we found at the end of the street were more sad streets.

"All the streets look the same," I said to my mother. "You'll get lost on the way to the pharmacy. Maybe I should go with you."

"Don't worry, Véro, I know the way," she said. "I'll cross the river at Pont de Sully, then turn left at Place de la Bastille. But if you think I can get lost, imagine how I worry about you! That's why I want you to wait for Francine after school. Never go anywhere without an adult and never without my permission."

As in Normandy, the blue, white, and red flag of the French Republic floated above the entrance to the public school. In the yard, amid a sea of strange girls, my mother found my new teacher, Madame Taraison, and abandoned me. Before walking away, Francine patted my head. "Be good, *mon chou*." Lots of French people called kids *mon chou*, my cabbage, but no one else ever called me that. No one but Francine. She added, "I'll be back at eleven-thirty to take you home for lunch."

Food was the last thing I wanted to think about. I needed to throw up or go to the rest room or both. Yet I kept this all to myself; I couldn't say a word to anyone.

The bell rang. Girls, all taller than me but all wearing school smocks like mine, surrounded Madame Taraison. She also wore a smock, perhaps afraid the kids would spill things on her. She lined us up two by two, hand in hand. A red-haired girl took my hand, and I kept my eyes on her feet. She wore leather shoes with straps, not muddy rubber boots like the farm girls in my class in Normandy. We marched inside and upstairs in tight formation behind the teacher.

When we entered the classroom, I read the blackboard: Write about your summer vacation. The Great Scholar was right! For the first time in days, I smiled. Thank goodness he had prepared me. Now I could get a good grade and start the year with a bang. Perhaps this new beginning wouldn't be so bad after all.

The teacher called roll alphabetically and sat us down one by one. I stood dead last, even though I was the littlest one. She called me Vo, Véronique, not Véro, and she placed me in the first row. In the front right corner of my wooden desk was a disc of white porcelain with a black hole in the middle—the inkwell. Its pure white was pristine, like my record at this new school; its circle was perfect like me—no goofs this time around.

The teacher gave each pupil a new notebook, a new pencil, a new metal pen point for our penholders, and a new sheet of absorbent paper to blot ink so it wouldn't smear. She gave them to me first, a sure sign of something.

All new things for a new me. She walked up and down the aisles with a dark bottle and filled the inkwells. Then she distributed sheets of lined paper and told us to write our essays.

I couldn't wait to dip my pen into the vibrant purple ink. I touched it to the rim of the well to let the excess flow back down. Then I wrote in cursive French what I'd practiced the evening before:

> *The airplane exploded in flight as I ejected. I searched the sky frantically for my copilot. When his parachute finally opened below me, it was the most beautiful flower I had ever seen in my life.*

I reread my paragraph. It was perfect. I loved my new school already.

I HOPED THERE WOULD BE no recess. In class I knew exactly what to do—sit with my hands together behind my back and be quiet. But the bell rang. Madame Taraison lined us up two by two, hand in hand. This time, she paired me with a blond girl. We walked downstairs in tight formation behind her.

She said *sh* every few steps, but nothing could stop the whispering along the way.

"I went to my grandparents'!"

"Me, too! Mine live in the North."

"We went to the seaside, and my parents took me to the beach every day."

Finally I figured out they were talking about their essays. *Oh, là là,* it didn't sound anything like what I'd written. *The airplane exploded in flight as I ejected?* What kind of a vacation memory was that? My legs got wobbly as I realized I was going to get a terrible grade after all. Would I be thrown out of school? My parents would be so ashamed! We might have to return to Normandy. What a mess—moving to the capital because my brother was too smart, moving back to my village because I was too dumb. I longed for that instant back when I'd first started writing, when everything was still possible, including success.

Some girls ran out in the schoolyard, while others stood around. One of them asked me, "What did you write about?"

I stared down at the blacktop.

"Maybe she doesn't speak French," said another girl. "She looks Chinese."

Of course I spoke French. And with no accent—not like my parents. I was French like everyone else. I just looked Vietnamese.

The girl raised her voice. "You!" She poked my arm. "Write . . . what?" She made writing motions in the air.

I blurted out, "I wrote that the airplane exploded in flight as I ejected."

Instantly the girls exploded in laughter.

"You made it up!"

"You're in trouble!"

"She's going to get a bad grade on the first day!"

"Stop it!" said a nice girl with long brown hair and pale gray eyes. "I like what she wrote. It's different."

The other girls lost interest and fluttered away. The nice girl took my hand and said, "You're Véronique,

right? My name's Sylvie." I squeezed her hand. She squeezed mine back. We walked between groups of girls who were jumping rope, playing hopscotch, or talking, inviting one another over on Thursday, when there was no school.

When the bell rang, Sylvie and I walked in line, holding hands. We got back in the classroom and Madame Taraison returned our writing. Going down the alphabet, she called one girl at a time to her desk, handed back each slip of paper, and announced the grade.

"Vo, Véronique." My heart pounding, I stood up and stepped forward. The gap between my desk and the teacher's might as well have been the English Channel.

When I made it to her side she handed me my page. I read my grade over and over again as she said it out loud, "Ten out of ten!" Then she added, "That was excellent, er, penmanship and grammar."

She had believed my explosion story! Maybe city kids flew in airplanes all the time and did jump out once in a while.

I walked back to my desk taller than before, smiling. Sylvie smiled back.

WHEN I GOT HOME AFTER SCHOOL, I showed my paper to Philippe. "It worked!" I said. "I wrote what you told me and got ten out of ten!"

"You did?" He stared at the page, wide-eyed. He must have been very proud of me. He looked shocked.

Nuts!

My new school wasn't so bad, really. Madame Taraison seemed to understand that I deserved attention, and the girls were friendly. Sometimes they were too friendly. One morning, about a week into the school year, my teacher walked up to two whispering pupils and said, "Enough!" She scooped something off of one child's desk and stored it in her own, adding, "You'll get it back at the end of the day. Playtime is over when you're in class." Then she tapped her desk with her ruler three times to obtain silence.

At recess I asked Sylvie what had got the girls in trouble.

"Chestnuts," said Sylvie. "Everyone collects them. Do you want to see mine?"

"Oh, *oui*," I said. "Where do you get them?"

"I pick them up from sidewalks and gardens, like everyone else," she said. "In the fall, they drop from trees everywhere in Paris."

Sylvie's chestnuts were glossy and maroon except for a big white spot. They ranged in size from as big as a walnut to as small as a pea. She let me pick two to start my own collection.

All of our classmates often compared chestnuts. Some lined them up from the biggest to the smallest to see whose row was longest. Some organized them into families: two large pairs for grandparents, one medium pair for parents, and small ones for the kids. The tiniest chestnuts got the most *oohs* and *aahs*. Sylvie showed me how the biggest were ideal to practice juggling. We rubbed our chestnuts clean on our clothes. We licked them to make them shine. We polished them with shoe polish. They were pocket pets to stroke in class while pretending to listen to our teacher.

"I used to make mini cows and horses out of chestnuts and toothpicks," said Francine one afternoon as she ironed sheets and pajamas.

It was a Thursday, so there was no school, which was great fun. I had all day to play with my brother, read, do anything I wanted. The only problem was that I couldn't see any of my friends. No school meant no Sylvie. I looked across the hallway toward the living room window, its sheer curtain lit up with sunshine. Why, why couldn't Sylvie and I go find another ton of chestnuts for our collections? Because I wasn't allowed to leave my apartment without a grownup, that's why.

"What's the matter?" asked Francine. "Do you need something? Tell me, *mon chou*."

"Could we go out now? To look for chestnuts? With Sylvie?"

"Let's find out," she said right away. "I'll call your mother at the pharmacy."

After she got permission, she called Sylvie's mother to invite Sylvie, and off we went. The ironing would wait until we got back.

"Philippe?" Francine asked.

"No thanks," he said. "I'll enjoy a break from Véro."

I began to squeal in protest, but Francine said, "He's

teasing you. Just get away from him."

She changed into her best dress, even though it wasn't Sunday. She was always ready to be discovered by a prince.

When we picked up Sylvie, she said, "My mother allowed me to invite you over next Thursday afternoon." Right away, I said yes, but Francine reminded me to ask my parents for permission.

Sylvie showed us the way to the Luxembourg Gardens. She and I ran ahead and picked up chestnuts to throw at things. The resident statues made ideal targets, especially their noses and other prominent body parts. We took turns smacking the stone kings and queens and watching out for the uniformed guards. We operated from behind trees to avoid getting caught.

Whack! I hit a statue right on the nose. That's when a whistle blew.

"Run!" I shouted. "Hurry!"

We fled without looking back. I grabbed Francine by the arm and yanked her off her bench. "Time to go home," I said.

On the way back, Sylvie and I walked ahead as if unsupervised. I was hungry and remembered the roasted chestnuts we used to eat as snacks in Normandy in winter. As they came out of the oven, we'd peel the shells off with our fingers, careful not to get burned. The meat was hot, mealier than a potato, and *mmm*, good! Roasted chestnuts filled us up and warmed us up. I said to Sylvie, "We don't really need any new chestnuts for our collections. Why don't we roast these and eat them?"

"Oh, no, I don't think they're that kind of chestnut,"

she said. "They don't look the same at all."

"I bet that's because we're used to seeing them cooked. These are raw."

"Maybe you're right," she said. "I'll roast one when I get home."

Francine and I left Sylvie at her apartment building and walked the rest of the way home. There, I asked Philippe if he'd like to eat a chestnut.

"These?" he said. "They're not the kind of chestnuts we eat. They're horse chestnuts. You can tell by the white spot. Horse chestnuts are toxic."

"What does toxic mean?" I asked. It sounded like a delicacy.

"In this case," he said, "toxic means if you eat it, you die!"

A chill froze me from head to toes.

"How much do you have to eat to die?" I squeaked.

"Just don't eat any, O.K.?"

My brother went back to his homework. I staggered down the hallway to where Francine was ironing. I held up the horse chestnuts, my hands joined as if in prayer.

"Is it true these aren't the kind of chestnuts we eat?"

"Yes," she said. "These are horse chestnuts. People often say chestnuts for short."

"Is it true that they're toxic? Like you eat them, you die?"

"Yes." She smiled. "You're a smart girl!"

I was smart to have checked, if only by accident. But was Sylvie as smart? Would she check with her mother?

Francine put away the ironing and went into the kitchen. From the hallway phone, I dialed Sylvie's number.

My heart was pounding so hard it shook me. The phone rang and rang, but no one answered. Where was everybody? Rushing Sylvie to the hospital in an ambulance with its siren blaring? I ran to my room and collapsed on my bed in the dark.

What if Sylvie was already dead? What if the police had started looking for her assassin? I didn't want to go to jail. It was bad enough not being allowed outside to play.

From his bedroom I heard my brother say, "It's too quiet around here. Where's The Sister?"

I said nothing.

He came to take a look. "What are you doing?" he asked. "Turn the light on!"

"I need to think," I whispered. "Leave me alone."

He shrugged and went back to his room. I wondered, should I tell him? But why? He'd laugh at me. He'd known all along about horse chestnuts. He always said he was a Great Scholar, and this would prove it.

Should I tell Francine? No. She'd said that I was smart. I didn't want her to change her mind.

The rest of the afternoon took forever to pass. At eight-thirty, my parents came home from the pharmacy. At the dinner table my father said, "Véro, you hardly ate anything and you haven't said a word."

"I bet she's getting constipated," my mother said. "She never eats enough vegetables."

I wondered if I should say anything. But what for? All they could do was call Sylvie's home. I could do that. So instead I asked about going over to Sylvie's the following Thursday afternoon. If, I thought, she was still alive.

"Why?" asked my mother. Sometimes she needed explanations for things that were obvious to the rest of the world.

"How?" asked my father. His question was reasonable, so he deserved an answer.

"Francine could take me there and back," I said. "All the other girls visit one another on Thursday."

My mother pouted. "You don't have to do everything French girls do." She used that line when she didn't feel like giving permission. It was a bad habit. This time she added, "I don't need another thing to worry about while I'm at work."

"Well, then," I said, "could Sylvie come here instead?"

"Not when I'm away from home," said my mother. "Just play with her at recess, O.K.?"

RIGHT AFTER DINNER, I called Sylvie again, but there was still no answer. Back in my room, I imagined being in school the next morning. I'd know as soon as the bell rang that Sylvie was missing. But Madame Taraison wouldn't know until roll call.

"Joulié, Sylvie," she'd say. "Sylvie?"

In my musing, all eyes turned to her empty desk. As our teacher marked her attendance list, the principal would walk in. My classmates would jump to their feet and stand at attention. The principal would whisper something to the teacher. The teacher would gasp, and tears would gush out of her eyes. Then the principal would make the grim announcement: "Something terrible has happened. Our dear little Sylvie has died, poisoned . . ."

Big gasps and cries would drown out the principal's voice. Would I be too petrified to cry? The grownups would notice, and that would be the end of me.

But it wasn't my fault! It was an accident!

Once that was established, I'd be forgiven. At the funeral I would sob uncontrollably. People would whisper, "Poor, poor little Véronique."

Then I'd brace myself, dry my tears, and sit up tall and stiff and admirable. People would stare at the martyr that I was, having lost my best friend at such a young age. Then they'd retreat in silence and in awe. And no one would make fun of me ever again.

I was brought back to reality when my mother poked her head in the door. "Bedtime!" she said.

"Can I make a call first?" I promised to be on the phone only one minute and dialed Sylvie's number once more.

"*Allô?*" said Sylvie's voice.

"You're alive!" I squealed. "You didn't eat the horse chestnut?"

"No," she said, "I checked with my mother first. I was about to call you. We just got back from my grandma's. She doesn't have a phone."

"You're not supposed to eat horse chestnuts," I said.

"And you can tell a horse chestnut by the white spot," she said.

After we hung up, I pledged never to eat another plant unless I was certain it was safe. To begin with, I planned to question my mother about the vegetables she served us.

My Gourmet Pet

Since I wasn't allowed to go over to Sylvie's and have a normal friendship, I needed a new friend in my own home. I wanted a pet who'd come when I whistled and lick my hand. But my mother would never allow a dog or cat because of the fleas. A goldfish wouldn't do. So I decided to tame a wild animal.

One Sunday morning we drove to the Bois de Boulogne, a park outside Paris. Beyond some lovely trees, their leaves red and green and gold, Philippe saw another boy flying a model airplane with a motor. He dragged our parents to join the crowd of spectators. That's when I went looking for wildlife under the bushes around a pond.

I saw lots of bugs and worms, but they were out of the question. Then I came upon a big snail. I picked him up. As he ducked inside his shell, I scurried to show him to my brother.

"A pet?" he said. "You mean, a gourmet appetizer. You're supposed to feed him nothing but flour for a week to clean his insides. Then we can eat him. Call him Two-Bites."

With a gasp, I ran away from Philippe. I put my snail in my skirt pocket and said, "Don't be scared. I won't let anything happen to you."

In the car on the way home, I asked, "What's for lunch?"

"Escargot," my brother said.

I jabbed my elbow into his ribs. He yowled, so my mother raised her voice. "Poached whitefish and fresh homemade mayonnaise. Francine made it in advance so it would be easier on me. Isn't that sweet?"

"Why did she make it in advance?" I asked. "Isn't she going to be there at lunch with us?"

"No," said my mother. "We can eat it cold. This is Francine's first Sunday off. Can you believe we've been in Paris a whole month already? She's spending the day with a friend."

"A boyfriend?" I asked.

My mother winked. "Francine said a friend, but you never know."

I'd heard Francine say that fresh homemade mayonnaise was the only kind real French people ever ate, and that it was also good on hard-boiled eggs or cold chicken. My mother always said that Francine made the best mayonnaise. My father always added, "But *Maman* cooks the best rice."

He tuned the car radio to *France-Musique*, the classical music station. It played a triumphant march to escort me and my snail through Paris.

After we got home, my brother came to my room, reading out of a cookbook, "Here's an escargot recipe: Stuff shells with garlic and butter. Bake in shell. Serve hot."

I was about to squeal when I remembered what Francine would've said, "He's teasing you. Just get away from him." So I reminded him, "You don't even know how to cook," and I pushed him out of my room and

closed the door. Like most French kids, I'd keep my pet snail in a shoebox and feed him fruit and vegetable scraps and flour.

"It's O.K. as long as he stays in the box and you keep it clean," said my mother.

I carried my shoebox with my snail in it to the bathroom.

"Here's some wet cotton just for you," I said. "I hope you like it."

Next I went to the kitchen.

"Would you like some lettuce?" I asked. "How about some apple and carrot?"

In one corner of the box, I added a plastic bottle cap with flour in it.

The snail came out of his shell. He stretched out on the cotton to enjoy as much wetness as possible. He extended his two tentacles, his eyes looking up at me from the tips. In his mighty presence, I held my breath. He was huge. I was thrilled.

I wiggled a finger at him. He waved his tentacles. I moved my finger closer. He retracted his eyes. I backed off. He made his tentacles longer again. He was calm now. I had tamed him. My patience had paid off.

He needed a name fit for a snail king.

"Thor," I whispered. "You will be called Thor."

My brother was going to turn green with envy. I carried the box to his room.

"Thor?" he said. "A better name would be Snack."

"You don't even like escargot," I said. "When *Papa* and *Maman* order that at the restaurant, you beg for pâté instead."

"You never know," he said. "There's a first time for everything."

I hugged the shoebox and changed the subject.

"Look how happy he is. Doesn't he look like a tourist on a beach towel?"

"Happy?" asked Philippe. "How would you know? No wild animal is happy in captivity. Maybe it's too wet— maybe he thinks he's drowning and he came out for air."

"That's not true!" I cried. "It can't be. He's a smart snail. If he doesn't like the wet cotton, he can crawl to the other side of the box."

Where was Francine when I needed her protection? Why did she have to have a day off? She could've taken me and my snail to the Luxembourg Gardens or wherever they had snail races. Snails were a lot like kids. It was no good for them to be cooped up all the time. That's why they came out of their shells to look around once in a while.

OVER THE NEXT FEW DAYS, Thor settled into his new home and lifestyle.

Like me, he loved the little yellow mirabelle plums that I picked out of the jar of jam. If I placed a piece a few centimeters from him, he went wild. He rushed to it. He draped himself all over it and made it disappear. But I was careful never to give him a piece larger than himself. He might have eaten the whole thing and exploded. When he ate flour, he powdered his whole front end with it. I'd wipe him clean with toilet paper. He never finished green peas.

"You're a gourmet like me," I said to him. "You don't like vegetables."

One day I put flour on my forefinger and held it near his flour dish. He looked at the dish, then at me, and he chose to come to me. When he reached to touch me, I found he was slippery and soft. Next I felt the gentle raspy strokes of his tiny snail tongue—scrape, scrape. He ate the flour off my finger. Was I the youngest person ever to be licked by a snail? He did it long after the flour was gone. Were these snail kisses? Could he feel the pulse of my leaping heart at my fingertip?

I wanted Thor to come when I whistled, like Zorro's horse on TV. I'd also seen on TV how animal trainers used treats as rewards. I decided to use mirabelle plums to train Thor, but only when my mother wasn't home. She believed girls shouldn't whistle.

Thor couldn't hear my whistle from very far, only when I got a few centimeters from him. Even so, he learned the trick fast. One whistle blow, and he'd race to me, obedient and eager. His reward was a bite of mirabelle plum.

Philippe had to see this. It would make him forget about model airplanes with or without motors. He'd die to have his own pet snail, faithful, loving, smart. A snail as talented as Thor was a ticket to fame and fortune. Thor and I could go on world tours to perform. I might even allow Philippe to come with us. Every kid on earth would want to be like me and my snail.

When I described my snail trick to my brother, he laughed.

"Everybody come, The Sister's Circus of Snails is coming to town!"

He danced around his room. I felt ready to dance, too—a war dance. But there was no need for that. Once I showed him Thor's trick, Philippe was silenced . . . for a few seconds. Then he asked, "Can I try?"

"It takes a lot of practice," I said. "You have to whistle just right, and you have to earn his trust." I gave Philippe a plum, knowing he would fail. But his failure would make my triumph greater.

Philippe didn't whistle. He just held the mirabelle a few centimeters from Thor. In slow motion, as in a bad dream, Thor pointed his eyes at the piece of plum. He slithered toward it and ate it.

Impossible! Philippe wasn't Thor's friend. Why would Thor obey anyone except me? He acted like . . . like an animal attracted to food!

"He's not coming because you whistle," said Philippe. "He just wants some mirabelle."

My brother's cackle rang in my head like shattering glass, piercing my heart. I couldn't believe Thor found anyone as special as me. The slimy traitor.

I ignored Thor for several days, and the next time I looked in his box, my heart skipped a beat.

"You look pale," I said. My head swam. "Thor, are you O.K.?"

His cotton had dried. Is that why he looked like a prune, or was I imagining it?

"Oh, no. Please, I hope you're O.K.," I whimpered, carrying the box to my brother's room.

"He's depressed," declared Philippe.

I knew the feeling.

My brother looked at my long face and at my sorry snail. "Why don't you release him?" he said. "He belongs in the wild. He can take care of himself."

"Are you sure?"

"Absolutely. He's a snail. What he needs is to go about his snail business in his natural snail habitat."

Smart people get second opinions, so I checked with Francine. She wouldn't pick him up, but she said, "*Oui*, good idea, release him. He'll be a happier snail. Much happier if he isn't in this apartment anymore."

So Philippe was right. I still wanted to keep Thor, but I wanted Thor's happiness even more. I wished I could be sure that he'd be O.K.

November first was coming up—All Saints' Day. My parents planned to leave Paris over the long weekend to go explore the Black Forest in Germany.

My father spread out a road map and showed us our route. "We'll go through the city of Metz, the mirabelle capital of the world," he said.

Then I knew what to do. I brought Thor on our car trip. Outside of Metz, I demanded that we drive around the countryside. Finally, we stopped in a hamlet so we could buy homemade mirabelle jam.

A few steps away from the road, I set Thor free on the edge of an orchard.

"*Au revoir,*" I whispered.

He waved his tentacles and crawled away in the grass under the mirabelle trees.

Kissing

After All Saints' Day, we went back to our usual routine. Every Monday, Tuesday, Wednesday, Friday, and Saturday, Francine would get me to school by eight o'clock, in time for class. At eleven-thirty, she'd wait on the sidewalk to take me home for lunch. Afterward, she'd walk me back to school by one. At four-thirty, she'd take me to the bakery to buy me an afternoon snack.

One day, I chose a bread with dark chocolate inside. I showed it to the cashier and was about to take a bite when she said, "Wait! You have to pay first."

Where was Francine? She should have been paying already. I turned around and found her standing just inside the door in the arms of a man.

"Madame," called the cashier, "please pay for this."

Francine and her friend smiled and came to the counter. He said to me, "Your snack is on me."

What a nice man! I looked at Francine to make sure it was O.K. Her eyes were on him, and she was beaming. She didn't even remind me to say thank you, but I did anyway. I guessed that he was her boyfriend, the one who had lunch with her on her days off.

"Why don't you choose a real pastry?" he asked.

What a treat! Normally, we only got real pastries on Sundays, after lunch. I put the bread back and chose a chocolate éclair.

As we walked home, Francine held my hand, her friend carried my satchel and her purse, and I ate my éclair. It took me awhile to finish it, yet by the time I was done, we still hadn't gotten very far from the bakery. What took so long is that they kissed the whole way. They reminded me of the horses I used to see in Normandy. They'd graze awhile, then take one or two steps and graze some more. Francine and her friend both bent their necks to the right and kissed each other on the lips. Then they took a few steps, bent their necks to the left, and kissed again.

My mother had told me that kissing and showing feelings was normal among French people. My parents and brother never kissed, but my best friend, Sylvie, kissed her parents good night, and I kissed my parents good night, too. They tolerated my acting French as if it wasn't my fault.

The slow walk home didn't bother me, because normally I wasn't allowed to play outside. Out here, fresh air moved freely. There were people to watch, shops to see. Passersby looked at Francine and her friend and smiled. Then they looked at me and smiled more. Everybody was happy—except my teacher, Madame Taraison.

On the opposite sidewalk, she stopped to watch us, frowned, and shook her head. She seemed upset. Maybe Francine and her friend weren't kissing quite right. They looked pretty good to me—maybe not as good as in the movies, but with practice they'd get better. A teacher should know that.

Perhaps she was bothered because she thought I was speaking to a stranger. But I wasn't speaking to him, and

he was no stranger. He was Francine's friend. True, I didn't know his name. To me, he was the Boa Constrictor, like the one I'd seen on TV. He kept one arm wrapped tight around Francine (the arm that didn't carry my satchel and her purse). Between that and kissing, it was a wonder she could breathe.

After dinner that day, instead of reading, I locked myself in the bathroom and practiced kissing the mirror. It was difficult, though, because when I bent my neck to one side, my reflection followed instead of going the opposite way. I could breathe while kissing, but my kissing experience wasn't genuine. I closed my eyes and felt my puckered lips getting smashed against the hard cold mirror.

THE NEXT DAY, AFTER SCHOOL, Francine and the Boa Constrictor offered me a pastry again. I wasn't too sure about that. I would have preferred a bread roll, but I did what the grownups wanted and picked a meringue.

When we walked out of the bakery, we went left instead of right, toward home.

"Where are we going?" I asked.

"A secret way, so your teacher won't stare at us," said Francine.

The secret way took us by the Roman arenas. As we walked, Francine noticed that I wasn't eating my meringue.

"Aren't you hungry?" she asked, glowing. "Then play. Run! Did you know that real gladiators fought here two thousand years ago?"

She went back to kissing the Boa Constrictor.

All that was left of the Roman arenas were a dozen stone rows next to an empty, round lot. The place was nestled between a solid line of tall apartment buildings and a half circle of grand old trees. It was quiet and peaceful.

I fed my meringue to the pigeons and sparrows. Then I ran in zigzags, chased by imaginary lions. I looked at Francine. Her eyes were closed, and she was still kissing.

I skipped along the lowest stone row, back and forth, faster each time. I glanced again at Francine, lost in her kiss. That's when I slipped and fell onto the edge of the ancient stone, bumping my knee. I cried out in surprise, and Francine raced to me. My red tights were torn, and my knee was dirty, but my skin was barely scratched.

Francine made sure I was O.K. and gave me a big hug.

After that, the Boa walked us straight home. Francine had me change into my pajamas, and she washed my knee to check again that it was O.K.

After dinner, I went to my brother's room to flop down on his bed beside him and his comic book. I stared at the airplane pictures. Then I asked, "Can we kiss on the lips?"

"Are you crazy?" he yelped as he bounced off the bed.

"I want to know if people can breathe when they kiss," I said.

"Who cares?" he shouted. "You're nuts! Get away from me! Go to your room!"

"I don't have to obey you," I said. "You're not a grownup." But I left his room anyway and went looking for Francine. I found her in the bathroom next to my parents' room. She had lowered the clothes drying rack from the ceiling above the bathtub and was hanging up my wet red tights to dry. My eyes met hers.

"What?" she asked.

I looked away. She got down on one knee and whispered, "What is it? I won't tell, I promise."

So I whispered in her ear, "Can you breathe while kissing?"

She blushed.

The door between the bathroom and my parents' room creaked open. My mother's face appeared.

"Why are you washing clothes at this time of the night?"

"I just washed Véro's tights," said Francine. She stood up and showed the tear at the knee. "I'll mend them tomorrow."

"What happened?" barked my mother, looming closer.

I backed up, bumped into Francine, and felt her hands on my shoulders.

"Oh, nothing," she said. "Véro tripped and fell at the arenas."

My mother gasped and started pushing up my pajama leg to see my knee. Then she glared at Francine. "You took my child *where* without my permission? The ar-renas? What ar-r-renas?"

I could tell my mother was upset, because her Vietnamese accent was getting thicker. The longer she r-r-rolled her Rs, the deeper the tr-r-rouble.

"That's cr-r-razy! You can't just take my little girl out and ar-r-round in this city. You two could've been kidnapped!"

"Oh, no! My . . . my friend, er . . . was with us—the whole time. He walks us home every day."

"Fr-r-riend? What fr-r-riend? You mean your boy-fr-r-riend?" My mother's eyes were bulging in unison with her thunderous Rs. "Go to the kitchen!" she ordered Francine. "I'll deal with you later. First I must tr-r-reat my child's injury."

"But . . . but . . . she didn't even break the skin!" said Francine. "It's true—look! And I washed it! With soap, as soon as we got home."

"Soap! That's no way to tr-r-reat a human child—like one of your cows! Br-r-ring me alcohol, surgical cotton, and Mercurochr-r-rome, r-r-right away!"

Francine quickly grabbed those items from the medicine cabinet behind my mother. She dropped the bag of cotton, and it took her two tries to pick it up. Yet she leaned toward me on her way out and whispered in a hurry, "The answer to your question is yes."

"Out!" cried my mother as she went to work on my non-wound. My knee hadn't even been bleeding before. Now it looked like a map of the Red Sea. She placed a bandage over it.

I went to bed promptly to get away from my mother, wondering if she'd make Francine do what she always made me do when I'd been bad—cross my arms, bow my head, and say *pardon*.

IN THE MORNING, I got dressed and went to the kitchen. My mother had sliced the bread. She was spreading butter and jam for everyone, swiping the knife with great force. She splashed a sugar cube and a spoonful of chocolate powder into my bowl of hot milk, then beat the mix with such energy that it foamed up.

"Fr-r-rancine won't be working here anymore," she declared. "She's going to be mar-r-ried."

"I know who she's marrying!" I squealed.

"How do you know?" asked Philippe.

"We must congratulate her," said my father.

"She's gone," said my mother. When she saw our blank stares, she added, "She's gone for good!"

My father and brother exchanged looks.

"Why?" asked one.

"Are you sure?" asked the other.

As soon as I was able to speak, I said, "But she didn't even say good-bye."

"Yes, why would she leave so suddenly?"

"Well, the r-r-reason is because I fired her," said my mother.

A complete silence followed. She was the one to break it. "She was socializing on the job."

I was quick to explain. "Her friend walked us home from school twice."

"She went off somewhere without permission," said my mother.

"The Roman arenas," I said. "Another way home from school."

"Not only that, but she took Véro! The nerve! So you see, she misbehaved, and she's going to get mar-r-ried anyway, so it was a perfect time to part."

But it wasn't perfect! And my father didn't think so

either. "You fired her for socializing? We could've just scolded her. What got into you?"

"I wonder that, too. What got into me when I *hired* her?"

"Normally we discuss important decisions," said my father.

"Well," said my mother, "there's not going to be any more spare time for fancy discussions. We have to take over all the housework. All of it, do you hear?"

Were they fighting? A chill flowed over my heart, and the bite of bread and jam turned sour in my mouth.

"Shouldn't we look for another maid?" asked Philippe.

"Oh, no!" said my mother. "No more maids. A maid is more tr-r-rouble than help. We'll get along fine without one."

"Who's going to clean the house?" asked Philippe.

"We will," she said.

My father gaped at her. "When?"

"After work."

"Who's going to take care of me?" I fretted.

"Philippe," she said.

Philippe stopped chewing, wide-eyed. My mother continued, "He may be twelve, but he's very adult, always has been. He's r-r-responsible enough to supervise you after school, Véro." She turned to my father. "They're good kids. They don't fight. They don't get in tr-r-rouble." Then she turned to me. "Obey your br-r-rother."

A smirk spread across Philippe's face and he nodded hard.

"Eat," ordered my mother, "or we're all going to be late."

After breakfast, I followed Philippe out of the kitchen.

"What will become of us?" I asked.

He shrugged. "I don't see a problem. I'm in charge. You obey me. Everything's fine." He gave me a long look and added, "*Maman*'s right. We don't need Francine. I can rough it. You won't hear me whine because my pajamas don't get ironed, as long as my shirts do, and *Maman* can do that."

When my mother came out of the kitchen, he asked, "Should I come with you now, so you can show me the way from her school to mine?"

"Not now! We're late."

She grabbed me with one hand, my satchel with the other, and charged out of the apartment, rushing me into the dark days ahead.

Mayo Wishes Come True

After Francine left, I wasn't allowed to play outside at all anymore, except at recess or on Sundays, at the Bois de Boulogne, the park outside Paris. My parents started taking us there every single Sunday, to make up for keeping us inside all week. But it didn't make up for losing Francine.

One time, as we drove home from the park, Philippe asked, "What's for lunch?"

My father glanced at my mother, then turned off *France-Musique* in a hurry. *"Sh!"* he said. "She's asleep."

"Is she sick?" I wondered.

"No, I think she's just tired from working all day then doing chores every night. She's not getting enough sleep."

"I have an idea," I said. This got my father's and Philippe's attention. "Let's give her a day off like Francine used to do. We can cook lunch so she doesn't have to."

"But who's going to cook?" asked Philippe.

"Papa, you can cook!" I said.

"Me?" he whispered.

"Oui!" I said. "At the pharmacy, you mix powders and things all the time to make pills for sick people. That's a lot like cooking."

Philippe shook his head. "It's nothing like cooking!"

"Doctors trust you, right?" I asked my father.

"This isn't such a good idea," warned my brother.

"Sick people get better," I said. "No one dies."

Philippe glowered.

After a silence, my father said, "You're right, Véro. And I know just what to make: French food. One of the simplest and most delicious French dishes. Cold chicken with fresh homemade mayonnaise. It'll be the best chicken you ever ate. Remember how Francine used to whip up a bowl of mayonnaise in the blink of an eye? I've read about it in the encyclopedia. The principle is quite simple."

Except for about a dozen dishes, we ate mostly Vietnamese food, like beef and noodle soup or stewed fish and rice. I was thrilled that my father was willing to act French.

We stopped at an open-air market to buy a raw chicken, then at the bakery for bread and pastries. We got home at noon.

My mother, now awake and informed of our plans, sat down in an armchair. I handed her a magazine. She held it in her lap but didn't open it. My father put on a record of beautiful, booming music. I sidestepped and twirled around the living room with my arms up.

"He was a lot like me, Borodin," my father said, "a scientist with a gift for art."

"Boro who?" my brother said.

My father motioned at the record player. "Borodin, the Russian who wrote this music, the *Polovtsian Dances.* Borodin was a doctor and a chemist who became a composer."

I wondered, would my father the pharmacist become a gourmet cook? Would he serve meals at tables on the sidewalk outside the pharmacy? Would he buy a restaurant? Maybe I could collect the dishes and wash them. Or write down the orders. I'd wear a pretty uniform and be my father's partner.

Philippe grabbed me by the arms.

"Stop spinning around. Come on, follow *Papa*." He pushed me into the kitchen.

"Mayonnaise," my father said, "is egg yolk and oil mixed together. It begins with one egg yolk at room temperature."

Philippe snapped his fingers at me and ordered, "One egg and the oil, quickly!"

My father said, "Let's cook the chicken while the egg warms up." He raised one finger. "It pays to get organized. That way lunch won't be late."

I thought of all the stars we'd get in the restaurant guide, especially the extra star for my neat uniform and for how well I'd take the orders. Philippe would beg to trade his model airplane for an apron. I would allow him to clear the dirty dishes from the tables. It would be his turn to get bossed around.

My father set a pot on the stove and watched it until the water boiled around the chicken. When the pot boiled over, he turned the flame down. He tried to clean the spill with a dishcloth. It started to burn, but he just blew on it and tossed it in the sink.

Philippe snapped his fingers and pointed at the window. I jumped to open it to clear out the smoke. Then I ran water on the dishcloth. I rubbed the burnt spot, but the black wouldn't come off, so I squeezed the water out of the cloth and folded the spot out of sight.

A while later, my father turned off the flame under the chicken pot. Then he touched the egg and nodded. He cracked it. Like a pro, he separated out the yolk, letting it slide back and forth between the two half shells. He moved over to the sink almost in time to avoid dripping the white on himself, the table, and the floor. He dropped the yolk in a small bowl.

Philippe snapped his fingers once more, glared at me, then pointed at the dishcloth with his chin. I wiped the table and floor, then put the cloth back in the sink.

My brother handed a fork to my father. I gave him a spatula, a tool fit for a pharmacist.

"A big spoon is what we need," said my father. "A fork might make bubbles, not mayonnaise. A spatula is too soft."

He broke the yolk with the tip of the spoon and moved it in circles in the bowl. With the other hand, he dribbled in a little oil. Yellow and clear stripes appeared. It looked nothing like mayonnaise. He moved his spoon faster, then slower. He added lots of oil. The problem got bigger. When he stopped the spoon, the yolk gathered at the bottom of a puddle of oil.

"You see why cooking is an art," he said. "Let's start over."

Perhaps there would be no restaurant—maybe just tables outside the pharmacy. And washing dishes in the back didn't sound so bad after all, especially if I could leave my brother out in front. Patrons would snap their fingers at him and expect him to jump for a change. I'd stay out of sight and out of trouble.

I shut the window and pulled the sheer curtains closed.

My father looked at me. "Don't worry. No one's going to come and arrest us for this." He emptied the bowl down the drain. He left the dirty dishes in the sink and took out a clean bowl and spoon.

My brother elbowed me.

"See how many eggs are left," he demanded, and when I said two, he ordered, "Get both of them out! Now! Do you want to eat today or tomorrow?"

While waiting for a second egg to warm up to room temperature, my father said, "We didn't get an emulsion."

"I thought we were making mayonnaise," I said.

"An emulsion," he explained, "is an oily and watery mixture so finely combined that it looks creamy. Mayonnaise is an emulsion. So are the ointments and lotions at the pharmacy, which I make all the time. Successfully."

My mother came in. As she surveyed the kitchen and sniffed the air, I held the dishcloth behind my back, and moved left and right to block her view of the mess. She looked at my father and shook her head.

My brother turned to her. "Can we start lunch with pastries?"

"Absolutely not," she said, and she walked out.

Philippe scowled at me. "Rich idea you had," he sneered. "It's so late we might as well start making dinner. This never happened with Francine. When she was around, we always ate on time. Look at us now! Never a decent meal anymore. And look at this mess!"

"I'll help clean," I said.

"Stop helping. You only make things worse." He walked out. I knew he and my mother would be sorry they'd missed the action. My father would succeed. He simply had to. He'd never failed at anything before. He was a good father.

Half an hour later, he used the second egg yolk. The miracle happened. In his magician's hands, at the tip of his spoon, creamy yellow swirls appeared in the bowl. He kept the spoon moving. With the other hand, he added oil drop by drop. Little by little, the bowl filled up with mayonnaise.

"Bravo, Papa!" I squealed.

I leaped to get the others to come see, but he said, "Wait!"

He looked in the bowl, down a very long face. As if alive, the mayonnaise squirmed into gross lumps. I didn't want it near me.

"Quick," I said, "throw it away."

He washed it down the drain, and what was left of my restaurant dreams went with it.

I kept an eye on the kitchen door, ready to yell, "Don't come in! I'll call you when it's ready," if my mother showed up again.

My stomach growled. I made a face. My father looked at the clock. It was one-thirty.

"Pastries first," he declared. He carried them to the dining room table. Even my mother ate hers without saying a word, not in French, not in Vietnamese. I was afraid she'd get mad about the spots on his shirt, but she just took a long look at them and sighed.

My father and I went back in the kitchen to the last egg. Then I had an idea.

"I'll be right back," I said, so he'd know that I wasn't abandoning him. I trotted to the closet outside his bedroom and found one of his clean white pharmacist's lab coats. I brought it to him.

"That's it!" he said when he saw it. "That's what we need! An emulsifier!"

"A what?" I thought I was holding a lab coat.

"An emulsifier would help the oil and yolk mix and stay mixed," he said. "Seeing the lab coat made me think of the science behind mayonnaise."

He put on his lab coat. "Emulsifiers are all around the house. In hand lotion, shampoo, toothpaste . . . H'mm . . ."

He stood deep in thought. Suddenly, his eyes grew wide. I knew a brilliant idea was forming in his great mind. "Toothpaste! Toothpaste is safe to swallow. I'll add a tiny bit to the egg yolk first."

And he was right. It worked! The yolk and oil turned creamy white, just like mayonnaise!

"Let's not tell *Maman* or Philippe how we did it," he said with a wink. "They'll never guess."

I beamed at him, then pushed the kitchen door open and shouted, "We did it! We did it!"

When the others joined us, my father said, "Who wants to try our mayonnaise?"

"Véro," volunteered my brother.

I tried just a little bit on the tip of my tongue. I closed my eyes and swallowed, then opened my eyes. "It tastes . . . good," I said quietly.

Philippe's finger went in the bowl, then to his mouth. His face fell. His tongue came out.

"What?" my mother asked.

"Mint!" he said, glowering at me as if I'd poisoned him myself. "It tastes like mint!"

My mother tasted it and frowned. "Your mayonnaise," she said, "tastes like toothpaste."

My father looked in the bowl and turned deep red. I worried that he might cry, but instead he laughed out loud and washed the mayonnaise down the sink. Philippe wasn't laughing, nor was my mother. I wished they would, especially her. I certainly felt a little like crying. I wanted my life back the way it used to be, back when I was the only one who did anything wrong and Francine cooked good food.

My tummy roared long and loud. At two o'clock, we wolfed down our chicken plain and cold.

I said, "I bet Borodin couldn't make mayonnaise either." No one said anything, so I added, "*Papa's* cooking will get better with practice."

My mother, who was washing down her chicken with water, choked a little. But when she got done coughing, she said, "No more practice. This is perfect. The best chicken I ever ate. Francine never cooked anything like this."

Joyeux Noël

On the last school day before the Christmas break, I began to feel a thick uneasiness in my stomach that had nothing to do with minty mayonnaise: our teacher had yet to make us write letters to *Père Noël*. In Normandy, we always did that during the week before the school break. Were people in Paris so busy they forgot? Not one girl in the class said anything about it. Yet they all talked feverishly about what they wanted for Christmas.

"Maybe a refrigerator for my doll."

"A doll with hair you can cut."

"Toys are for little kids," I declared. "I think I'd like a book, just like my big brother." He wanted instructions on how to make a model airplane with a motor.

At the end of the day, when I said good-bye to Sylvie, I asked her to call or write.

"I'll write you a letter," she said, "when I'm at my grandparents in the country, after Christmas. You write back."

"O.K.," I said. "Isn't there another important letter to write?"

"I don't know—is there?"

"To *Père Noël*?" I whispered.

"Oh, yeah." She giggled and ran to catch up with her mother.

At home, I sat at my wooden desk with a blank page and a pen: *Paris, 21 December,* I wrote. *Dear Père Noël* . . . I reported that I'd been pretty good all year and made sure to describe my change of address from Normandy to Paris. Then I put my pen down.

I owned only one doll that was larger than my hand. She'd lost all the eyelashes from her right eye, which no longer opened. If I didn't ask for a better-looking doll this Christmas, who knew? I might go through life without one. The next year, I might be expected to act more grown-up and really ask for a book, as my brother did. I went to show my unfinished letter to him.

"Is nine the right age to stop asking for toys?" I asked. "At what age am I a big girl?"

"You . . . a big girl?" Philippe exploded into laughter. He closed his eyes. He snorted. Then he panted, "*Imbécile!* You still believe in *Père Noël?* It's *Papa* and *Maman* who buy gifts for us every year," he howled. "They put them out on Christmas Eve after we go to bed."

"It's not true," I said, melting into tears. I ran to my room and slammed the door, holding my letter against my heart and sobbing. Was there no jolly *Père Noël* with a basketful of toys on his back, walking along roofs and climbing down chimneys? Deafening thoughts rushed around my skull. The room spun around me. My brother was so mean! His laugh echoed in my head like mad. And my parents—I wasn't about to ask them about this. If Philippe was right and they were merely pretending, why should I believe them now? If only Francine was still around. She could have told me what French kids thought. She never would've laughed at me. I missed her terribly, especially now that I had no one left to go to.

After a while, I ran out of tears. I got ahold of myself and made a plan to find out the truth about *Père Noël* without risking more ridicule. I buried my unfinished letter in my desk.

THAT EVENING, to kick off the holiday season, we had a French dinner: white veal sausages dotted with black truffle bits, mashed potatoes, and applesauce. Best of all, my father didn't cook.

In the middle of dinner, my mother said, "I'm going to take tomorrow off from work. We'll go to the flower market to buy a Christmas tree."

I squealed with delight. "They have Christmas trees in Paris? Just like in Normandy?" I regretted having spoken, because I was sure Philippe would make fun of me—but he didn't. His mouth was full.

My father said, "And I'll take off the day after. I'll take both of you to the *Galeries Lafayette* department store to see nothing but toys!"

This time, I was careful and kept quiet. How many toys could there be? In Normandy, all the toys in town filled one shelf at the village hardware store. It took five minutes to look at them twice. I glanced at my brother. He didn't protest being dragged to see toys at the advanced age of twelve and a half.

THE NEXT MORNING, my mother drove us to the heart of the city. *Père Noël* was painted on shop and restaurant windows everywhere. I took great care not to mention him so Philippe wouldn't bug me about it—but all he talked about was how tall a tree he wanted. The market was on one of the two islands in the river Seine. My mother allowed us to pick a tree as tall as Philippe, one that didn't cost too much. When we got the tree home, we set it up in front of the unused fireplace and spent the afternoon trimming it.

But the lights on our tree were nothing compared to the glory of the *Galeries Lafayette,* where our father drove us the next day. The department store stretched along several blocks. It was near the Paris opera, and millions of lights twinkled across the nearby shop windows and boulevards. A plastic *Père Noël* hung in the middle of the street, far above traffic. The sidewalk was covered with kids. The crisp air echoed with their cheerful voices. Every giant store window was a toy display. This would be, I suspected, better than the hardware store in Normandy.

One window held a Lego castle the size of my bedroom, with animated knights on horseback. In the next, dolls dressed in richly colored velvet with lace and ribbons danced to pretty music. Next were toy cars on a mini freeway, roaring and honking. Child-size mannequins were at play, dressed as musketeers and princesses, astronauts and dentists.

Inside, we went up the grand staircase, around a Christmas tree several stories tall, to the fifth and sixth floors, where there was nothing but toys. At booths and tables, grownups handed out toys so we could try them out. Children roamed free, and their parents followed them.

I stopped in front of dolls with coats over their dresses.

"These are for big girls," the store lady informed me. "Be careful not to break them."

I wondered, but not out loud, Am I a big girl? I looked at the lady. Maybe she knew who came to get the toys for kids, parents or *Père Noël*. Maybe she didn't. I didn't ask.

I reached for a doll twice as tall as my hand was long. Her eyelashes were longer than mine. She smiled a little, and she smelled so good! Her dress had pink and white stripes and pink bows, and her pink corduroy beret matched her coat.

"She's beautiful," I said as soon as I could speak.

I looked over my shoulder for my father. He was right there. I caressed the doll's curls, her face, her dress.

We explored the toy floors for hours. Twice I went back to that doll, buttoned her coat, and straightened her beret.

To tear us away, my father promised to buy roasted chestnuts from a street vendor. I checked them for white spots, to make sure they weren't toxic. We shared them in the car on the way back.

At home, I pulled out my letter to *Père Noël* and wrote at the end, "the doll in pink." Then I shoved it back inside my desk.

WE HAD CHESTNUTS AGAIN BEFORE LONG, with our Christmas Eve feast. On the dessert platter, a tall pile of mandarin oranges, each with a leaf still attached, looked like a tree covered with shiny ornaments.

After dinner, Philippe and I each selected a pair of shoes to put in front of the fireplace—that's where *Père Noël* would leave his presents. With a rag, I wiped my largest shoes, my sheepskin winter boots. Then I looked at my best shoes, the shiny black ones. Should I choose the bigger ones, which had more room? Or would *Père Noël* frown at their scratches and stains? I wasn't about to ask Philippe. I chose the shiny black pair and put them next to my brother's, behind the tree, on the marble slab in front of the hearth. The fireplace was closed by a black iron panel because we never made a fire—none of us knew how. It was just as well. I didn't want *Père Noël* to risk burning his toes.

I wondered why Philippe put out shoes if he didn't believe in *Père Noël*. Did my parents make him do it because of me? Or was *Père Noël* real? At bedtime, I kept my door and my eyes wide open in the dark. If *Père Noël* came, I didn't want to miss him. And if my parents carried presents to the living room, I wanted to catch them in the act.

THE NEXT THING I KNEW, I woke up with a start. My door was closed. Daylight slanted through the metal shutters on my window. It was Christmas. How could I have missed my chance to see who brought the presents? I jumped out of bed and raced to the living room.

My brother had already found his present on his shoes and opened it. It was the book that he wanted, the one about model airplanes. It was a good book, I thought—one that would keep him away from me all day, maybe for several weeks.

My good black shoes had disappeared under a gift box. Inside was the doll in pink. She looked like a dream. Her wavy hair was golden, her ponytail fluffy and bouncy. Deep in her gray-green eyes, I found a promise of good times together.

I picked her up, ran to my parents' room, and shook my mother awake.

"Joyeux Noël," she mumbled. "What did you get? A doll! Why, she's gorgeous. Isn't she too warm? Take her coat off." Then she rolled over and went back to sleep.

THAT DAY, I SPENT EVERY MINUTE with my new doll. I wanted to show her my letter to *Père Noël*, so I looked for it everywhere in my room.

My mother poked her head in. She had bags under her eyes, but she was smiling. "What are you looking for?" she asked. When I told her, she said, "Oh, I mailed it for you the other day. Come on, lunch is ready. There's a mocha yule log for dessert."

Afterward, I took my new doll to my father in his armchair. I sat her on his knee. He put down his science magazine, took my hand, and made me caress my doll's curls, her face, her dress. Who gave me this doll? *Père Noël*, who did get my letter after all, or my parents, in which case they weren't likely to confess?

Then Sylvie called.

"Joyeux Noël!" she said. "My parents bought me a crib for my doll. They said I could take it to my grandparents' tomorrow. What did you get?"

"A doll." I swallowed and made myself say, "My parents bought me a doll."

"That's great! Have you named her yet?"

I couldn't believe I hadn't. By the time we got off the phone, I'd named her Bénédicte.

LATE THAT NIGHT, I SAT UP IN MY BED and listened in the dark. It was quiet. I pushed away the warmth of my sheet and blanket. Holding Bénédicte on my heart, I left my bedroom and ventured down the hallway. From the street, dull light came into the living room through the slits in the metal shutters. I tiptoed to the Christmas tree and lay down on my side under its branches, on the marble slab in front of the fireplace. Behind the tree trunk were the wooden legs of the coffee table and armchair. They looked like a forest. On the ceiling, plaster angels were stuck smiling permanently. They didn't care. They didn't worry when the wind moaned down the chimney, rattled the iron panel that closed the fireplace, and found a way in through the bottom crack. Icy air licked my shoulders.

I rolled onto my back on the hard cold marble. The clock was ticking on the fireplace mantel. My first Christmas in Paris was over. It tasted salty, like tears.

I shivered. It was all because of the cruel breath of winter flowing down the chimney. It came from the roof where no *Père Noël* had ever walked with a basketful of toys on his back.

I kept my weeping silent. My heart was swollen. After a while, I closed my eyes and took a deep breath. The Christmas tree smelled good, like a magic forest where nothing changed unless I wanted it. I took another big breath. It smelled like Bénédicte, my beautiful

new doll. I hugged her tight, filling my hands with her soft hair.

Bénédicte was born in Paris, where the lights and toys were fabulous. She could tell me what other wonders this city had to offer. In exchange, I'd show her how glorious the holiday season was in our family—her family now.

The festivities had barely started. My mother would serve French holiday foods for days. On the first of the year, we'd all sit in front of the TV and watch the orchestra in Vienna play happy waltzes. My parents would take more time off work to spend with us kids and take us on special outings. Too bad Sylvie was going to her grandparents' in the country after Christmas— otherwise I could've asked for permission to visit her.

My parents! They worked so hard to take care of us, spending all day at the pharmacy and then doing chores every night. They deserved to have their fun. Philippe was all grown up, and no little brother or sister came after me—I was their last chance to pretend that there was a *Père Noël*. Maybe I could do it one more year, just for them. I might even enjoy it.

I lifted Bénédicte up and took her back to bed. "Sleep tight," I whispered. "And sleep quick so it's morning soon and we can play. *Joyeux Noël!*"

Dream Remnants

Bénédicte enjoyed playing. She was a glamorous doll, a Parisian doll, and she liked to look her best when she was playing. She needed a new dress, something other than her everyday, pink striped one. One peaceful Thursday afternoon, while my brother was in his room, I had time to sit down with her. I helped her take off her dress, then I examined it. The front and back were sewn together along the shoulders and down the sides. The back closed with a snap. I could make a dress like that.

At my desk, I placed the dress on a piece of paper. With a pencil, I traced lines all around it.

With Bénédicte in one hand and my drawing in the other, I went to my parents' bedroom. I found a pile of fabric remnants on top of my mother's sewing basket. There was itchy wool from pants and skirts she'd shortened. Too plain. And there was an old shirt with the buttons cut off so they could be reused. It was made of boring striped cotton. Underneath was—I couldn't believe my eyes—one of my mother's blouses, the white one with the multicolored flowers all over it. It was the kind of blouse that goes on over the head and closes behind the neck with one button, but the button was missing. My mother must have cut it off to save it, as she'd done with the striped shirt. This fabric would make a beautiful dress for Bénédicte. It was happy like summer, bright like her.

I gathered scissors, a needle, and red thread and carried it all to my brother's room. I showed the blouse to him and asked, "Can I use this for my doll?"

He barely glanced up from his homework. "Sure, do what you want."

I spread the blouse on the wooden floor and smoothed a spot big enough for Bénédicte's dress. I put my drawing on top and cut through the paper and fabric, along the lines.

Philippe looked up. "Hey, stop that!" he said. "You're getting bits of thread all over my floor! Quit making a mess. Go to your room and stay there! I don't have time to watch you."

I went back to my room to sew the dress along the shoulders and sides. Then I cut the back open. Done!

I put Bénédicte's arms through the arm holes, but though I pulled hard, the new dress was too small and wouldn't close in the back. I wondered what to do—start over or fix it? I didn't want to redo all the cutting and stitching, so I decided to add a cape. Attaching it to the dress on the shoulders would hold everything together. I used two safety pins. A good breeze would lift the cape and cool Bénédicte's back through the wide-open dress. This new look would be all the rage next summer.

I put Bénédicte in my bed with the covers up to her chin. I didn't want her to be seen until I was ready to surprise everyone with my hidden sewing talents. As a hot new fashion sensation, I had to be introduced to the world properly—maybe on TV, gliding down a grand glass staircase to the sound of trumpets and applause. I'd

hold Bénédicte and be dressed exactly like her in a
magnificent gown signed *Véronique, Paris.*

I walked out of my room to go put the remains of
the blouse back on the sewing basket, only to bump
into Philippe, who said, "Didn't I tell you to stay in your
room?"

"I need to put this back."

"Well, hurry up," he said. "Then go back to your
room and stay there."

"What if I need to go to the toilet?" I asked. "Can I
have permission to do that? Or do I have to ask for your
permission to come ask for your permission?"

"Stop it," he snapped. "And don't make me wait."

By the time my parents got home from the pharmacy,
I'd decided that Bénédicte's new dress needed a touch
of lace.

I followed my parents into their bedroom as they
talked about the day in Vietnamese. While they changed
clothes and chatted, I looked through the sewing basket.
I held up a package of lace. "Can I have this for my doll?"

My mother looked at it from across the room. "No,"
she said, switching to French. "We don't use new things
for dolls, only remnants."

I put down the lace and picked up a bunch of ribbons.
Ribbons of different colors might go well with the
flowers.

Philippe walked in with something in his hand.

"This shirt lost a button," he said.

"Leave it on top of my sewing basket," my mother
said.

Lace, I decided, not ribbon. That would make the dress truly special. I held up three different bits of it. "Can I have this?" I asked.

"Choose one," my mother said.

The longest bit was narrow, and the middle bit stiff, but the shortest was wide, detailed, and soft—the most special. That's the one I chose.

Back in my room, it took me some time to make up my mind about where to sew the lace on the dress. My mother called everyone to the dinner table.

"Can I just finish one thing?" I hollered.

"After dinner," she answered.

At the table, I looked at my parents and brother, their heads bobbing up and down to meet their chopsticks. They had no clue what was about to happen. The world would come to our door to interview a Véronique they never knew lived among them. Their lives—our life together—would change forever. This was what the parents and brother of a soon-to-be famous designer looked like in the final moments before fame. Philippe would have to learn to treat me better.

After dinner, I sewed the lace on the dress and ran to my mother.

"Look, *Maman*," I said. "I made a dress for my doll."

"You made that?" she said. "How pretty, how elegant, and the cape! Ooh, I love the fabric."

"I knew you would," I said.

"Isn't it the same as my favorite blouse?"

"*Oui,*" I said.

"How clever! Where on earth did you get it?"

"From the remnant," I said.

"What remnant?"

"The old blouse on top of your sewing basket."

"You mean my blouse? The one that just needed a button sewn back on?"

"It was a remnant," I insisted. "It was with all the other remnants on top of your sewing basket."

My mother took a deep breath, touched her forehead with the back of her hand, and laughed.

"What's this?" she said. "Philippe's idea of a joke? You talked *Papa* into taking you to buy the same fabric, right?"

I said nothing. Her smile disappeared, and so did mine.

"Stop it," she said. "This isn't funny."

My silence made her scowl.

"Tell me r–right now where you got the fabr–ric!"

"I told you already."

She spun around and rushed to her room. I followed.

She held up her blouse with its giant hole through the front and back. She gasped, then cried out several times, *"Oh là là,"* as if the hole were through her own heart.

Desperate, I whimpered, "It isn't my fault. *You're* the one who mixed it with all the other remnants."

Then she exploded. "You're a bad, bad girl! Cr–r–ross your arms, bow your head, and ask for forgiveness!"

Her voice sliced through me, and I wondered if she was going to spank me. Sylvie got spanked when she'd been bad. For once, I was hoping that we wouldn't be

too French. I repeated through tears and sobs, *"Pardon, pardon."*

"Now go to your r-r-room and stand in the corner. But first, pr-r-romise you won't ever again take anything from me without asking."

"But I did ask!" I cried. "I asked Philippe. He said it was O.K."

My brother poked his head in the door.

"Sounds like The Sister goofed really big," he said.

"It's all your fault!" I shouted, and my mother ordered, "Go to your r-r-rooms, both of you!"

From my room, I heard her lecture him. "You're supposed to call when you have a question."

"But I didn't have any question," he protested. After a silence, he added, "You take Véro to the pharmacy after school. See for yourself how much trouble she is."

"The pharmacy is no place for a kid," she said.

"Then why did you fire Francine? I can't do everything around here. How am I supposed to keep an eye on Véro and get my homework done?"

Alone in the corner of my room, I cried softly for what seemed like forever. I thought about sewing my doll's dress back into the blouse, but I knew there was no way.

At bedtime, my mother came and caressed my head.

"Cry no more," she said. "It wasn't your fault. You asked for permission."

But her words only made me cry all over again, so she took me in her arms and rocked me back and forth.

We sat down on my bed. "It's O.K. to make your doll dresses from remnants," she said, "but you must ask me first about every single piece—fabric, lace, anything."

"When?" I whined. "You're never home. You're always at the pharmacy."

"Call me there!" she said. "Like Francine used to whenever she had a question. She would've known better than Philippe."

"You're right!" I said. "With Francine around, none of this would've happened. She would've sewn the button back on your blouse already. . . ."

". . . and the button on Philippe's shirt," continued my mother. "You're right."

We sat looking at our toes.

"You know what?" she started. I sniffled and looked at her. "Francine called me today," she said, "to thank me for the wedding gift I sent her. Sometimes I wish I hadn't fired her. I wonder if I overreacted."

I knew the answer to that, and I knew better than to say so.

"Is she married?" I asked.

"Yes, and she lives in Paris with her husband. She's looking for part-time work."

I thought of Francine, my protector, keeping Philippe away from me, letting me out to run free, and taking me to Sylvie's. "Did you ask her to come back?"

"No," said my mother. "I'm not sure we need her. Normally you two are good kids. You don't fight. You don't get in trouble. What happened to my blouse is the exception that proves the rule."

"Ask Francine to come back," I said, "quick, before she takes another job! Ask her to take me to Sylvie's one Thursday afternoon."

But my mother said, "You play with Sylvie twice a day at recess. Isn't that enough?"

I didn't think it was.

"You need to be serious sometimes," she said. "The first priority in life is duty."

"Please, let's call Francine and ask her to come back," I coaxed.

It took my mother a minute, but she said, "No . . . I don't think we need her. What we need is to keep trying."

My face must've fallen halfway to the floor. I could tell by the way she looked at me, as if she wanted to console me but didn't know how. Maybe I could help her with that. "About the remnants," I said, "what if I had my own? You could approve them now, but I wouldn't use them until later. I'd keep them in my room."

"I like that idea," my mother said. She gave me a shoebox, approved several fabrics, and added two needles and two spools of thread.

"Will you pick a remnant from your shoebox so we can make a dress together on Sunday?" she asked.

I nodded. She put her arm around me and smiled, and I smiled back as I looked into her eyes. She didn't know it, but I planned to make a dress big enough so she could wear it.

Eagle White

My mother declined my generous offer to make a dress for her. After we'd made one for my doll, I went back to keeping my brother company.

"Back off!" he growled. "This is fragile."

I slipped away from his side, leaving him bent over the model airplane he was building.

"Don't you need help?" I asked.

"What I need is for you to get out of my hair," he said. "I've waited all my life to build a motorized plane. Now it's going to take forever because I have to watch you all the time."

He measured a wooden stick and marked it with a pencil, but he pressed so hard he broke the lead. With a sigh, he sharpened the pencil back to a point.

"I thought you liked being responsible," I whispered.

"What makes you think I mind? Responsibility I can handle," he assured me. "I just wish you'd move out of my way and back into your room—stop causing disasters left and right. I never have any quiet time anymore. No time to read, no peace, and now look! Here I am again, talking to you instead of finishing the most important airplane of my life!"

He squeezed glue from a tube, but too much came out, so he glared at me as he cleaned up the mess. He put one drop on each end of his wooden stick and pressed it in place.

"You're in charge," I said. "Can't you call Francine and ask her to come back? Then she could watch me and you'd be free."

"I only have control over you," he said, then he scrunched up his nose and added, "if that."

"We could tell *Papa* and *Maman* that my teacher said to get Francine back. They're so busy they'd never check!"

"You'll have to think of a better plan than that."

"We could go on strike like grownups. We could make signs and march around the dining room."

"No, no, no. It's not a good idea to tell parents what to do. It's better to let them figure things out for themselves. I'll have to think of something. I will."

I knelt down, folded my hands over the edge of the desk, and parked my chin on top of them. I looked up at him, a twelve-year-old grownup. I wished my parents could see that he was old enough to supervise me outside, maybe even take me to Sylvie's.

After he completed the airplane's wooden frame, he let the glue dry overnight. During the next few days, he covered the frame with rice paper. Within a week, he added a motor and a propeller from the hobby store.

He gave his flying machine a name in English, *Eagle White*. I didn't speak English, so he translated it into French for me.

I sighed. He lived in a world above mine. He was learning a foreign language at school. "Will I ever learn English like you?" I asked.

"You know some English," he said. "You know *Eagle White*."

THE NEXT SUNDAY MORNING, our whole family went to the Bois de Boulogne. Philippe brought *Eagle White,* his toolbox, and a small can of fuel. A little boy ran over and stood right next to us to watch as Philippe poured the smelly fuel in the plane's tiny gas tank. After several starts failed, he got the motor running. The little boy's parents pulled him back, but they stayed within the growing circle of spectators. Keeping his fingers away from the propeller, Philippe turned a screw and tuned the motor until its high-pitched roar sounded just right. The noise attracted more people.

Philippe handed *Eagle White* to our father and backed away in small steps, unwinding the pair of nylon strings that was attached to the plane. I followed Philippe, but he nudged me away. Still, I lifted my face and looked around so everyone in the crowd could tell whose sister I was. My hair was jet black like Philippe's, and like his, it was perfectly straight.

I sat on my heels and reached into the toolbox. My brother looked at me and shook his head. I ignored him and moved the tools around, pretending to look for something. Everyone could see that I was allowed to touch the marvelous stuff because I was part of the *Eagle White* team. The little boy reached in the box.

"Don't touch," I snapped, startling even myself.

"O.K.," said Philippe, and my father launched the plane. It flew in circles around my brother. He pulled on one string and the plane flew upward a little.

"Oh," whispered some people.

He pulled on the other string and the plane flew downward a little.

"Ah!" said the audience.

He made the plane loop-the-loop.

"Bravo!" cheered the crowd.

The plane flew around many more times until it ran out of fuel. My brother let it glide toward the ground and landed it smoothly. Everyone clapped, and the applause sounded like fireworks. The air was tingling with sparks of excitement.

THERE WERE MORE GLORIOUS FLIGHTS that day and again the following Sunday morning. Each time *Eagle White* took off, so did I. With it, I swooped down to the grass tips, surged toward the sun, and looped-the-loop, so free, ready to shout.

Some spectators talked among themselves. I knew they wondered who this genius was, this Vietnamese boy who piloted his plane like an ace. And I knew they couldn't wait to see his sister do it.

"Is it my turn yet?" I asked my brother.

He gave me a quick glance.

"Can't you just watch? This isn't for little sisters."

"Can I help at all?"

"Look," he said, "I don't want anything to happen to my plane. I think I would die."

All I could do was breathe down his neck while he refueled, fiddle with the tools, and watch *Eagle White* fly until my chest was ready to burst because the sky couldn't fit inside it. I asked again and again to fly the plane.

Finally Philippe said, after a landing, "O.K., you can bring it back to me. But be careful!"

I raced to the plane, and putting my right hand under its belly, I lifted it above my head and jogged back. All eyes were on me. The air rushed under the plane's wings and gave it a little lift. I tightened my grip and ran faster and felt all the eagles on earth soaring in me.

Not until I delivered *Eagle White* to my brother did I see it: my thumb, buried in the plane's belly, hooked around the wooden frame through a hole in the rice paper. I held my breath, my soul suspended in midair. As my brother recovered his treasure from me, I freed my thumb. I couldn't tell which was the bigger dark hole: the one in the plane or my brother's mouth, wide open in a silent cry. Then he squeaked, "What did you do?"

"Nothing," I said to save my life.

"What do you mean, nothing? *Imbécile!* You poked a hole in my plane!"

"I didn't do it! It was there when I picked it up!"

Spectators turned their eyes away. Philippe shrieked at our parents, "She wrecked my plane!"

"I'm really sorry," I whimpered. I crossed my arms, bowed my head, and said, "*Pardon, pardon*, Great Scholar."

Parents began to drag their children away, but the children kept staring back at us.

My brother's voice went up an octave. "She can't do anything without causing disaster!"

"It was an accident," said my father. "It will be simple to fix. She wants to be like you, to hold an airplane.

You're almost thirteen, you should know better. Next time, don't let her handle something fragile. That's asking for trouble."

"But she's such a pain!"

"She's your little sister."

My mother said, "It's time to go home. I have to make lunch and I have a lot to do after that."

But my brother slumped on the grass and whined, "It's not fair! I want to be a little sister so I can get away with breaking things."

IN THE CAR, PHILIPPE AND I both tried to tell our versions of what had happened, but our voices were squashed by my father. My mother slept most of the way. After we got home, our voices flared up again, but my father demanded silence, so Philippe slammed his bedroom door shut. I waited. Nothing happened. I stood there awhile, wanting him to reappear and yell at me or laugh at me so I could fight back. Time passed. What was he doing in there? Inventing instruments of torture in just my size?

At lunch I tried to tell my parents on him, but he raised his voice to drown mine. My father said, "What's with the two of you? You never used to fight so much."

"It's normal for kids to fight," said my mother. "I used to fight with my br-rothers, and not just with words!"

My father lowered his voice. "In my family, we talked things over like civilized people."

"Oh, is that where you got it?"

"Got what?"

"All talk, no action," she said.

"What's that supposed to mean?"

"You could help ar-round the house once in a while," she said. "Or did your family do no more than philosophize about cooking and cleaning and eating and getting dr-r-ressed? Maybe you never got dr-r-ressed, since you never did anything!"

"Even Francine got Sundays off from Véro," snarled Philippe under his breath.

I had a lot to say, but I didn't have the heart to add to the argument. We never used to fight like this, back when Sundays were happy days.

Monsters

After lunch, Philippe said, "Wait till Sylvie hears how clumsy you are."

"It wasn't my fault," I said. "It was an accident."

"I'll tell her tomorrow morning when I walk you to school," he said.

I protested, "You don't need to tell her anything."

He carried on energetically. "And I'll tell your teacher. I can hear your whole class laughing, *har, har, har!*"

"You don't have the right!" I cried.

"You don't have the right!" he parroted in a high voice.

"Don't you have a plane to fix?" I pushed past him, holding my chin high.

He snorted. "Nine years old on paper but still a baby in real life!"

I spun around and stomped my foot. I was boiling inside. When he acted like this, talking to him was like making conversation with a motorized pogo stick. It didn't pay to be reasonable, yet I had to do something to make him stop. But what?

What I really wanted to do was play with my doll, help her put on her coat and take a walk around the apartment. But with Philippe the way he was, I knew he'd just keep making fun of me. I wasn't going to give him that chance. So Bénédicte and I sat in my bedroom and read a book of spooky stories.

"Véro's a baby!" nagged my brother.

I was trapped, unable to make him go away, unable to get away from him. But I knew one thing—sooner or later, even the meanest brothers have to go to the toilet. Then I'd be free from him, my burden lifted, if only for a few minutes. Free to get even.

Through my open door, I watched Philippe. Time passed. Finally, he walked to the rest room at the other end of the hallway. As soon as the door closed, I raced to his room and looked all around, wild with hope. I leaped to his desk, where *Eagle White* sat with its thumb-sized hole. I flung every drawer open. There were colored pencils arranged by shade, model airplane parts in neat rows, and glue bottles and tubes with their brands in alphabetical order. I was tempted to break some things, but I didn't want to confirm that I was clumsy.

There was a stick of licorice. I licked the whole length of it, waved it around to dry it, and put it back. I bet he could never tell. From the back of the bottom drawer, I grabbed a small toy airplane, a really old one that was all metal, dating from the time before he made models. I also took a spool of clear nylon string before closing the drawers. I didn't yet know what to do with these things, but I'd think of something. I wasn't clumsy. I was clever.

Back in my room, I rushed with trembling hands to hide the plane and string under my pillow. The plane fell on the floor and bounced under my bed. I reached with one foot to get it back. It scraped across the wooden planks, giving me an idea.

I tied the string around the plane and put both under my pillow. Bénédicte looked on with a gleam in her eyes.

The toilet flushed. I jumped back in my chair with my book and Bénédicte on my lap. The rest room door opened, and my brother reappeared. He spoke, so right away I spoke louder.

My father hollered, "Quiet!"

Yet Philippe mouthed silently, *"Imbécile!"*

I was shaking so much it took me two tries to close my door, but when I did it, I slammed it so hard that I startled myself. My brother's door echoed mine.

My mother shouted, "No slamming doors!"

Then we heard my father again, speaking slowly in a low voice, "I said, quiet!" We knew better than to anger him any further.

I'd show Philippe. I could learn to be sneaky, too, with a genius like him teaching me. All I needed was for him to go to the toilet once more.

I waited and waited, but Philippe didn't go to the toilet again all afternoon. Finally, I went to the kitchen to pour a big glass of apple juice and carried it to his closed door.

"Excuse me, Great Scholar?" I chirped.

Not a sound, but when I turned the knob, the door opened, so I walked in.

"I brought you some juice," I sang like a lovely bird.

He glared at me but drank it up.

I was no pharmacist, yet I knew that what goes in one end comes out the other. Half an hour later, he headed for the toilet. I carried the toy plane with the string tied around it back to his room. I pulled some string off the spool and threw the toy under Philippe's bed. It skidded to the wall with a *thunk*. I peered under the bed and saw it in the far corner. It had landed upside down as if after a crash. Then I unwound the clear string and stretched it from his bed to the door and around to my room. I made sure it ran along the floor, invisible, then stuffed the spool under my pillow and locked my door when the rest room door opened.

THAT NIGHT, I WAITED for the snoring from my parents' room to get good and loud and for the breathing from my brother's room to get deep.

I pressed one ear against the wall that separated me from Philippe and pulled on the nylon string a little. There was a rumble—the metal toy bouncing along the wooden floor under my brother's bed. Then bedcovers wooshed and springs creaked. I froze, holding my breath. He must have sat up. There was another creak as he lay down again. I dared to breathe and suppressed a giggle.

After his breathing grew deep, I pulled on the string again and again and again. Then I couldn't resist yanking it with all my might, rising until I stood on my bed, my arm up like the Statue of Liberty. The toy plane must have hit the foot of Philippe's bed, because the scraping ended with a loud *clank,* followed by his cry of terror.

The nylon string went limp. The knot around the airplane must have come untied. Quickly I wound the string around my hand, then buried the evidence under my pillow.

85

I heard Philippe jump out of bed, throw his door open, and run to my parents' room. Their door burst open and a light switched on.

"Papa! Maman!" shouted my brother. "There's something under my bed!"

My parents' bed squeaked as if in alarm or in sympathy for Philippe's bed.

"Come quick!" pressed my brother in a high voice. There were muffled words.

I poked my head out my door just in time to watch them shuffle to Philippe's room in a single line, my mother groaning, my father yawning, my brother following last. As soon as he passed me, I said, "Aren't you a little old to be afraid of monsters under your bed?"

Philippe was back at my door instantly, his arms stiff, his fists clenched.

"It's not monsters," he said. "It's real! There's something under my bed growling and knocking."

The more I giggled, the more he fumed.

In Philippe's bedroom, my father muttered in Vietnamese, "All this for a bad dream?"

My mother said, in French, "O.K., we're here. What's the problem now?"

He went to answer her. I followed, skipping and trumpeting, *"Twelve years old and afraid of monsters under your bed? Wait till I tell your friends. I can hear your whole class laughing, har, har, har!"*

"I'm telling you, there's really something down there," Philippe insisted.

My father was on his hands and knees, reaching around under the bed.

"There's your monster," he said, holding up the toy airplane.

"Stop calling it a monster," said Philippe. "You're driving me nuts! I never said anything about a monster." He stomped his foot.

"You must have kicked it under by accident," grumbled my father between yawns, "and it got dragged by your bedcovers."

"Enough about monsters under the bed," my mother said sharply, and she walked out. "Back to sleep. You, too, Véro."

My father also walked out. "Can't even get a good night's sleep since Francine left. I want her back!"

Philippe chimed in, "So do I!"

"Me, too!" I sang.

"Back to bed!" my mother ordered in a tone that did not invite conversation. She marched away with my father in tow.

But I wasn't finished with Philippe. "They have picture books to help little boys who are afraid of monsters," I offered, my voice dripping with honey.

"Be quiet," he said.

"Be quiet?" I said. "Now, there's an idea. How about you be quiet, and I'll be quiet. If you never tell anyone about the hole in your plane, I'll never tell about you and monsters."

"But . . . but you can't . . . why would anyone believe you?" he tried.

"*Papa* and *Maman* believed me right away," I snapped. "You heard them. They both think you're scared of monsters."

He scowled, his shoulders up and tense. "O.K. I won't tell if you won't."

What a deal! I went back to bed with a smile so big it felt like it went three times around my head.

Secret Agents

The next afternoon, after school, Philippe poked his head in my door.

"Agent 009?" he said.

I wondered, what now? Was he coming to be nice to me or to boss me around? I gave him a blank stare.

"Say yes, and call me Agent 008," he said.

"What do you want?" I asked.

He walked into my room. "Can I have some fabric?"

From the floor, he picked up my shoebox of fabric remnants. I jumped up, yanked it from his hands, and said, "What are you going to do with it?"

He glanced left and right. Why? Our parents were at the pharmacy.

"I know how to make *Maman* want Francine back," he whispered.

My mouth dropped open. No wonder he was in a good mood.

"If you promise not to say anything," he said, "I'll tell you more."

I nodded and leaned toward him so I wouldn't miss a single word.

"I've got it all figured out!" he continued. "A trick we can set up so *Maman* will see for herself that she needs Francine. It's time to cause some trouble. No more good kids."

Philippe's ideas were always the best.

"I need your fabric to make this work," he said. "Please?" His eyes were glued on my shoebox. "You can come along and watch, 009. Can I have some fabric?"

"O.K.," I said, "but only if I get it back."

He promised, so I let him choose several pieces. "I wonder how many I'll need," he said.

"Take the whole box," I suggested.

He stopped to look at me as if for the first time. "Good idea, 009! You might make a good spy."

I handed him my remnants and saluted, "*Oui*, 008!" Then I asked, "Why are we 008 and 009?"

"Because I'm the next best spy after James Bond, 007," he explained.

He flipped up his shirt collar and tucked his neck down, then pressed his back against the wall and tiptoed away. I did the same. I followed him as he carried my box to my parents' bedroom and closed the door behind us. He headed straight for the alarm clock, which my parents kept far from their bed, on a chest of drawers across the room. They didn't want to risk oversleeping, and this way they had to get up to turn the alarm off when it rang. They never wanted to be late for work because in life, duty came first.

I wanted to observe Philippe's every move, but he said, "Watch for enemy spies."

"What enemy spies?" I asked.

"Do it," he said. "Secret agents always cover each other, like James Bond and his buddies in the movies."

He was counting on me! I opened the door just a crack and pressed my ear in the opening, but turned my head so I could see what 008 was doing. Like buddies,

he said! I would never let him down now. Nothing would escape me—not a sight, not a noise, not the smallest hint of imminent danger.

Philippe held up two pieces of fabric, red wool and striped cotton.

He rolled up the red one, pushed it inside the alarm clock's bell, and said, "This one should fit better."

"No, it's too thick," I said. "It'll fall right out. Use the other one, 008. It'll stay rolled up right where you put it."

He tried it and nodded. "You're right. You sure know your fabrics. It was pure genius on my part to bring you along."

He *was* a genius. He could imagine things and make them happen. He got them right the first time, not like me. He was headed for a perfect life and he was taking me along.

He stuffed fabric into the bells and pushed it up so it couldn't be seen.

"See, they set the alarm for six-thirty," he said. "Let's test it."

"Good idea, 008," I said.

He made the alarm go off. Instead of ringing loud and clear, it sounded like an old goat with a sore throat. We giggled in unison.

"I get it," I said. "Great trick, 008."

He turned the alarm off and set it back to six-thirty. I would have forgotten to do that. Philippe always thought of everything. He wasn't even thirteen, and already he was a master spy. Would I ever be that smart?

"Check everything," he said. "I'll take a turn covering you."

Me? Check on my big brother's work? I marched across the room with my chest out and my chin up so high that I could hardly bend down to look at the clock.

"O.K., 009," he said, "mission accomplished. We're out of here."

He pulled me from the room, but I looked back. "My shoebox!"

It was still on the chest of drawers. He went to get it. "You saved us," he said. "Now, back to our rooms, and act casual."

I stuck my hands in my skirt pockets and strolled back to my room, whistling.

"Stop," he said. "No whistling. It's too obvious. Get your hands out of your pockets. Now walk." Philippe was overdoing it again, but I obeyed him anyway. Back in my room, he asked, "Can you learn a secret code?"

Of course I could. I could easily do anything for 008, and better than anyone.

"Secret agents need a secret code," he said, "for secret messages, like at dinner, right in front of *Papa* and *Maman*. So they won't have a clue about our mission."

"How?" I asked. "They'll see us passing notes back and forth."

"No notes," he said. "Spies have to eat their notes, *pouah!* Let's use gestures. If I rub my nose with the back of my right hand, it means 'help!'"

I mimicked him, then added, "If I scratch my eyebrow, it means 'pretty funny, huh?'"

"And if I close my eyes long enough to count to three," he said, "it means 'quiet!'"

We practiced our secret code. Then he said, "Now remember, let's act natural when *Papa* and *Maman* come home, O.K.?"

I looked at him with my eyebrows lifted.

"We'll act like we're not in cahoots," he explained. "No glances, no winks, no giggles, O.K.?"

"Shouldn't they at least know that there's something they don't know?" I asked. "Otherwise, where's the fun?"

"No, no, no!" he said. "This isn't a game. Promise you won't say a word, no matter what happens."

"I promise." There was nothing 009 wouldn't do for 008.

"Remember," he said, "silence. Fellow spies would die for one another."

Oui, I couldn't wait to jump out of burning airplanes into runaway trains to rescue him.

AT DINNER, I TRIED NOT TO SMILE too much. Were my parents staring at me above their chopsticks? Did I look like one giant muzzled wiggly tongue?

At one point, I had trouble lifting the water pitcher to refill my glass. I remembered the code, so I put down the pitcher and rubbed my nose with the back of my right hand to ask 008 for help. It worked! He poured my water. We were a great team!

At bedtime, I went to sleep wondering if my brother would grow up to be a famous spy like James Bond. That would make me a famous spy's sidekick. One day,

I'd sacrifice myself to save him, and then I'd be his idol for the rest of his life. Or maybe he'd save me in return.

NEXT THING I KNEW, I woke up to a furious knocking on my door. When it burst open, my mother's voice hollered, "Get up! Now! We're all late for everything."

I staggered out of my room, rubbing my eyes. My mother dashed across the hallway while my brother ran by in the other direction, putting on his shirt. My father sat in the hallway chair, frowning while putting on his socks and shoes. He smoothed his messy hair with both hands and said to my mother in Vietnamese, "We'll be about an hour late opening the pharmacy. We'll miss some clients."

She cried out loud. I couldn't tell if it was Vietnamese or French.

I hurried to the kitchen and swallowed some food, then rushed back to my room and grabbed some clothes without quite waking up. In the hallway, my brother was dressed, satchel in hand.

"Go to school," my mother said to him. "I need to speak to your sister."

He stood there with a puzzled look on his face.

"Go!" she said.

Philippe walked out the apartment door, but I didn't hear his footsteps go down the stairs.

My mother turned to me. "Look at you, so innocent, so sweet, like a little angel. Who would think you're capable of such practical jokes?"

I wondered what she meant. I knitted my brow and raised my sleepy eyes.

She exploded. "Look what we found inside the bells of the alarm clock. Fabric! Your fabric r-r-remnants!"

She handed them to me. But I hadn't done it. Philippe had. And I'd promised I wouldn't tell, no matter what. The time had come to prove myself.

"This is called being caught r-r-red-handed!" shouted my mother. "I've had enough of your tr-r-rouble. Enough! Enough! Enough!"

Her yelling hurt my ears and rang in my skull. I started to cry. I wanted to tell her Philippe had done it! Just a few words could end this instantly. But they'd also end my brother's trust, maybe forever. All I saw was my mother's angry face, her mouth so mad, so loud. This was how fellow spies died for one another—no burning airplanes, no runaway trains. Just one spy, alone with the enemy while the other escaped.

Suddenly my brother's voice squeezed in between my mother's shouts. "Stop! Stop!" he said, pulling her sleeve. "Véro didn't do it. I did. It's my fault. It's me you must punish."

My mother's mouth stayed open, but the noise stopped. She grabbed Philippe and pulled him into his room, where my father joined them. I listened as he scolded my brother in a low voice slowed by anger.

"Cross your arms," my father said. "Bow your head, and ask for forgiveness. When you get home from school this morning, stand in this corner until lunchtime."

I planned to stand at his side, my lovely brother who had sacrificed himself to save me, my Philippe, my hero forever.

My mother reappeared. She picked me up and held me to her heart and said, "I'm very, very sorry I yelled at you. *Pardon*. I should've gotten the facts first."

Then came my father. "Why are you crying, my little one?" he asked.

I didn't know anymore, so I held up my fabric and blurted out, "It's all wrinkled."

Minutes later, I figured out why I was still crying, but my father never asked again. It was because my big brother had made a mistake. His life was no longer perfect, and he wouldn't get a second chance. For him, it was all over. Not only that, but even my mother had made a mistake.

My father said, "Let's all get in the car. We'll drop Philippe at his school, Véronique at hers, then we'll go to work."

That's when my mother said, "And I'll call Francine. Maybe she can come back today!"

I turned to Philippe. We exchanged wide-eyed looks with our mouths hanging open. We didn't need a secret code for *hurrah!* We skipped down the street, arm in arm.

At the car, my father said, "Philippe, everybody makes mistakes. What matters is that you learn from them."

I listened so hard that my ears stretched. My father continued, "If you're smart enough to imagine how to stifle an alarm clock, you should've thought of the consequences. Yet you told the truth, knowing you'd be punished. That takes courage. You make me proud."

I couldn't believe it. My father, too, could see that Philippe was a hero!

My mother nodded. Philippe looked at her and opened his mouth.

"Quiet," she said.

So my father said to her, "Fix your coat, will you? It's buttoned all wrong—as the French say, you buttoned Monday with Tuesday."

I opened my mouth, but my father said, "Quiet."

So I said nothing about his socks—one brown, one black.

In the back seat of the car, Agent 009 scratched her eyebrow—pretty funny, huh? Agent 008 closed his eyes long enough to count to three—quiet!

Little Sparrow

When Philippe and I got home that afternoon, we immediately called my mother at the pharmacy to find out why Francine hadn't shown up. "She's at her parents' farm. She'll be back Wednesday night and she'll come over all day Thursday." In two days! I was beaming, and I could tell from my mother's voice that she was, too.

I asked her, "Can Francine take me to Sylvie's on Thursday afternoon, please?"

My mother sighed. "You must want it badly. I guess it's O.K."

Yes! It was a dream come true: finally, to act normal, like all the other French girls. Philippe and I were buddies, Francine was coming back . . . I couldn't think of what else to wish for, except Thursday.

I called Sylvie, and we thought of a hundred games to play. After I got off the phone, I stood in the hallway, living in advance of Francine's glorious return. I'd show her Bénédicte and her new dresses, tell her all about my adventures since last fall, and how Philippe and I did things together all the time now.

Philippe had gone back to his room and was whistling a happy tune. I walked to his door. He got up from his desk, came to me, whistling and skipping, and without a word, closed the door between us.

It took me several seconds to react. Maybe this was a new game. I knocked on the door.

"Don't come in!"

Toc, toc, toc. "Hey, 008, it's me, 009." I wished he'd tell me how to play this new game. I was ready for new games together.

"I said, keep out!" he barked.

"Great Scholar?"

Silence. Was he mad at me? It made no sense.

I thought we were buddies. What had I done? Maybe it was because I'd licked that stick of licorice in his drawer. I would've asked for permission, but he was in the rest room at the time. When a big brother is in the rest room, it's a dangerous time for all his things. Maybe it was because he was afraid I'd tell about the monsters under his bed. But we had a pact of silence! I hoped that he hadn't changed his mind about holding up his end of it.

I shouted, "You're not supposed to keep your door shut!"

"Stay away! There's top secret stuff going on in here."

What was he up to? I thought secret agents had no secrets between them.

He said, "I need peace to get something important done."

"I'm going to tell." The door stood closed and silent, so I drifted back to my room and closed my eyes. Would Francine's return mean going back to when Philippe and I weren't buddies? I felt an emptiness in my tummy.

MY PARENTS CAME HOME EARLY THAT NIGHT, laughing, planning the last two dinners before Francine's arrival.

They sounded like little kids. Good thing no one could hear them. And Philippe! He emerged from his room and added plenty of giggles to their silliness.

I grabbed his sleeve. "Now can I go in your room?"

He turned to me, his face smug. "No."

"Why?"

"I don't have to explain anything to you if I don't feel like it."

I wanted to cry, but I didn't want him to call me a baby.

For dinner, we had cold boiled chicken, though not with mayonnaise! We had it the Vietnamese way, with steamed rice, the zest and juice of a lemon, a little salt, and slivers of onion. It was supposed to be with lime juice and minced lime leaves, but there were no limes in France. For once, my mother was happy to make a simple meal, willing to give herself a break and giddy over Francine's return. "I feel like I'm about to get a vacation," she said. All she'd had to do was to give it to herself.

No one noticed that I couldn't smile, not even my father. Usually I loved boiled chicken, but that night I didn't feel like eating. I put hot rice in my mouth, chewed it, and swallowed it slowly, hoping it would warm my heart. If only Philippe would allow me in his room again. Like when we were secret agents and best buddies. Like just that morning. I wished I could hold on to the passing minutes, stop drifting farther from when everything was O.K.

My father said, "You know, I could make this some time. How could anyone mess up lemon juice?"

"We believe you," my mother said. "No need to prove it."

WEDNESDAY AFTER SCHOOL, Philippe closed his bedroom door again, but after a couple of hours, he opened it. I ventured in, and he didn't shoo me away. He said, "Come look."

I walked to his desk, my feet hardly touching the wooden floor. The last two days melted away like a bad dream. I wasn't sure they had even happened. My head swam with relief. It took me awhile to realize what I was looking at.

Eagle White had been repaired, the torn section neatly cut away and a patch of rice paper glued over it. And there was a new airplane made entirely of wood. While my brother put the finishing touches on it, I found myself breathing down his neck again. "Why did you use wood instead of rice paper?" I asked.

"It's stronger," he said.

The new airplane had a red propeller and was powered by a rubber band instead of a motor. On each side was a label in English. "How do you say that?" I wondered.

"Little Sparrow," read Philippe.

I mouthed the words silently, unable to imitate the foreign way he rolled the Ls and the Rs. So I said, "It doesn't sound nice."

"But it is," he said, and he translated it into French for me, *Petit Moineau.*

I smiled. "Oh, I like it."

He placed *Little Sparrow* in my hands. I was stunned that he would let me touch it. I held it for a few seconds

without closing my fingers, then gave it back to him.

"Keep it," he said. "I made it for you. It's your reward for being such a good secret agent."

I was speechless. So this was what he'd been doing. How could I have thought he'd abandon me? I should've known. We were buddies! He was the best brother.

He and I sat on his bed, holding *Eagle White* and *Little Sparrow*. Together we flew in formation. He coached me on how to make airplane noises.

I wanted to do something extra special to say thank you. I decided to make a card and surprise him. I wanted it to last forever, but I didn't have wood to use, so I piled on layers of paper and glue, paper and glue.

That night, when I presented the card to my brother, he read,

> *Cher Philippe,*
> *Merci pour* Little Sparrow.
> *Véronique.*

He took a good look at the card. "It's really thick. It must have taken time. Nice work."

Beaming, I pranced back to my room. Seconds later he screamed, "Who used up all my glue?"

Going Bananas

On Thursday, Francine brought homemade straw-berry jam for breakfast. Cheers rose around the kitchen table.

"Véro," she said, "look at you! You're a big girl now. I missed you, *mon chou.*"

I jumped up to kiss her on both cheeks. Everything she said sounded like a song to me. My mother hugged her and kissed her and went to work happy.

All morning long, Bénédicte, *Little Sparrow,* and I followed Francine around, except when she vacuumed and took the trash downstairs. I stayed away from Philippe. After I used up his glue the day before, I wasn't sure he'd allow me near him, and I didn't have the heart to find out. Why couldn't all of life be O.K. at the same time?

In the afternoon, Francine got ready to walk me to Sylvie's apartment. "Philippe?" she asked.

"No thanks," he said. "I'll enjoy a break from Véro."

I began to squeal in protest, but Francine said, "He's teasing you. Just get away from him."

He said no more. He watched us go down the stairs and still hadn't closed the apartment door by the time we walked out of sight.

AT SYLVIE'S APARTMENT, Francine repeated to me, "Remember your manners," and rang the doorbell.

Noisy steps echoed my racing heart. It was my first visit to a friend—and a French home—in Paris. The door opened to the greetings of Sylvie and her mother, Madame Joulié.

While the grownups shook hands, Sylvie and I kissed on both cheeks. Then she said, "*Bonjour,* Madame," and shook Francine's hand.

Francine squeezed the back of my neck, making my face blurt out, "*Bonjour,* Madame!" Then she pushed me forward and said, "I'll pick Véronique up at five."

After the door closed, I noticed a little boy wrapped around Madame Joulié's legs. He had brown hair like Sylvie's, and like hers, his eyes were pale gray like a winter dawn.

"That's Sébastien, my little brother," said Sylvie.

Her mother said, "Go play." Then she headed down the hallway, and to my great relief, Sylvie went the other way, followed by Sébastien and me.

"Are you from the Chinese restaurant?" he asked. "Is your home red and gold? Does it smell good like sweet and sour pork?"

Sylvie turned around and said, "She's not Chinese. She's Vietnamese, well, her parents are. Véro was born in France, just like you and me."

"So you're French," he said with a smile.

I nodded and smiled back. Then I caught up with Sylvie.

She walked into a bedroom with two beds and two desks. Philippe and I had always had our own rooms. I thought parents were the only kind of people who shared a room.

Sylvie opened the tall, narrow window. The breeze swirled in. It carried the smell of the pink roses from a vase on the chest of drawers near the window.

Sylvie stepped up on a chair, grabbed a shoebox from the top of the armoire, opened it, and said, "Look at my treasures."

Among them were horse chestnuts from the previous September! I reached for the nuts, but Sébastien took my hand and dragged me to his desk.

"Look at my notebook," he said. He showed me drawings he'd made with colored pencils.

"Write something," he pleaded.

"He always wants attention, especially from guests," said Sylvie, rolling her eyes.

I picked up a green pencil and wrote: *Sébastien slurped strawberry soup.*

"Your turn," I said. "Recopy what I wrote, a whole page of it."

He obeyed instantly. Amazing! Did I have that power, the same power that Philippe had over me?

Sylvie and I spent time looking at her books, many of which I also had. She let me pick one to borrow.

Then we sat on the wooden floor, and she took two medium horse chestnuts from her shoebox and handed one to me. With a pencil, she drew a smiley face with round eyes on the white spot. I used the pencil to draw a smiley face on my nut too, except with slanted eyes. With a nail from her shoebox, she poked four holes in her nut and pushed in toothpicks for arms and legs. We giggled and did the same with my nut.

"I can write!" trumpeted Sébastien as he plunked

his notebook in my lap, spilling the nuts on the floor. He'd drawn line after line of squiggles and zigzags— mini worms with a serious case of the giggles.

"Ah!" I said, pretending to be impressed.

"That's good, Sébastien," said Sylvie. "Now draw a picture, a very big picture." She winked at me.

Instead, he begged me. "Read to me what I wrote."

I glanced at Sylvie in distress. What was I to read, worm, worm-worm, many mini worms? She mouthed at me, "Just make it up."

I looked at what I had written on the page earlier, "Sébastien slurped strawberry soup." I read it out loud three times. Then I said, "Go sit on your bed and read it in your head." He obeyed.

What a simple thing it was to be in charge! For me, anyway. A gift, that's what I had. I wondered why Philippe always made such a big deal about being responsible for me.

Sylvie and I picked up our horse chestnut dolls. We made them kiss on both cheeks.

Sylvie said, "Let's be best friends forever."

"Oh, *oui!*" I said. "I hope we always live in Paris so we can play together."

We used a piece of tape to help the dolls hold hands. Then we ran to Madame Joulié to show them to her, and Sébastien ran after us.

Sylvie's mother took us to the kitchen for an after-noon snack. We each got a slice of homemade apple tart and a glass of grape juice. I envied Sylvie because her mother was always home, even though I liked it better when her mother was in another room. Then I could relax.

When done eating, I carried my plate to the sink. Madame Joulié started doing the dishes. She massaged a little dish soap all over her diamond ring to work it off her finger. After she finished the dishes, she put her ring back on.

Sébastien walked around the table and leaned on me.

"Eat a banana with me," he said.

I didn't want more food, but I needed to maintain his grand opinion of me.

"O.K. Let's split one."

"I'm not supposed to use a knife," he said.

"Who needs a knife?" I said. "Just break it in half."

"How?"

Sylvie and her mother both stared at me. I was surprised that none of them knew. At home I did this all the time. I grabbed a ripe banana, wrapped each hand around it, thumb against thumb, then bent the banana away from me: *r-r-rip!*

Sébastien laughed out loud. His mother clapped, and Sylvie said, "What a great trick!"

Then she had to try it, so she and her mother shared a banana, too.

"Me, too! Me, too!" chanted Sébastien.

"No, no, that's enough," said his mother. "No more banana."

He whined a little, but her frown quieted him.

Sylvie finished her half banana and went to the bathroom. Madame Joulié opened the window and waved at someone down in the street.

"I need to speak to you," she called out. "I'll be right down." Then she said to Sébastien and me, "Go back to the bedroom and play," and she left the kitchen.

Sébastien reached for a banana.

"You can break bananas later," I said.

He nodded and dashed out. I followed him.

In the hallway, he said "Wait," and went back to the kitchen. When he reappeared, he yanked on my sleeve and pulled me into the bedroom. He reached out the window and touched the black paint on the wrought-iron railing.

"This is new," he bragged.

"Maybe the paint is, but I bet the iron rails are almost a hundred years old, like your building."

"That's not true!" he said.

"It is, too," I said. "The year that the building was completed is engraved in the stone wall. 1894."

"Where?"

"Outside, just under the balcony."

"I want to see it! Let's go down to the street."

"We'd better ask your mother for permi—"

He hopped up and bent his waist over the railing. I grabbed the seat of his pants. "No-o-o! Don't! Don't lean over the railing, O.K.?"

"O.K.," he said.

Cries of "*Oh, là là,* the bananas!" came from the kitchen. I hurried there. Sylvie stood shaking her head, staring at the whole bunch of bananas, each broken in half. Sébastien! He must have done it when he went back to the kitchen. Was this my fault? I'd told him he could break bananas later. I didn't mean all of them, one minute later!

"Quick, put them back together before your mother sees them," I said. "Match up the halves. Look, you can tell the straight ones from the curved ones."

With trembling hands, we started to group the half bananas into two piles, straight and curved, and I tried to match them back together, mashed and less mashed. Sylvie helped.

"Do you have strong tape?" I asked. I had to fix this mess. Otherwise Sylvie's mother might never let me visit again, especially not when she had ripe bananas around. And in Paris, you could get ripe bananas all year! Sylvie opened a drawer and took out a roll of packing tape.

"Too bad we don't have yellow tape with brown spots," she said.

That's when screams came from her bedroom. We abandoned all the half-fixed bananas and raced down the hallway.

There was Sébastien, wailing on the window sill, his head stuck between two iron rails.

"Oh, no!" I cried. "What a nightmare!"

Passersby began to gather and stare at the commotion.

"I'll get my mother," whimpered Sylvie.

I heard her despite the racket that her brother was making and said, "No, we can free him before she finds out. Help me."

Sébastien's head had made it through the rails on the way out, and it hadn't gotten any bigger. It had to go through the rails on the way back in. The problem was that his ears were catching. His piercing cries made me cringe, yet I reached through the bars and pressed his ears flat against his skull.

"Pull him back," I yelled at Sylvie.

My fingers got pinched, so I let go, and his ears caught on the railing again.

I begged Sébastien. "Be quiet, or your mother will hear you," but my words had no effect.

Down in the street, his mother ran out of the building, looked up, screamed in unison with him, and ran back inside.

I hollered over Sébastien's voice, "Sylvie, please, help me free him before your mother gets up here."

"We need something even skinnier than your fingers," she hollered back. "Something thin, to hold his ears against his skull."

"Tape!" I yelled.

Sylvie rushed away.

Her mother exploded into the room and shrieked out the window, "Help! Call the fire department!"

In response, she got free advice from the street below: "Call the police!"

"No, no, there's no immediate danger."

"Stay calm, everybody."

"The silly boy just needs a little help."

Madame Joulié yelled, "I'll call my husband," and flew out of the room.

Sylvie came back with packing tape and scissors. She cut one long piece. With it, I taped Sébastien's ears tight against his skull. I wanted an extra piece for his mouth—he made so much noise—but I didn't think Madame Joulié would like that. I pulled Sébastien's shoulders back. His screams turned into a moan. The crowd started to clap, but next came a chorus of disappointment, and again Sébastien's voice grew loud enough to crack the stone walls. It hadn't worked. Why not? Maybe on the way out, his earwax had helped his ears slide through the railing, like the dish soap had helped Madame Joulié's ring slide off her finger.

Soap!

I raced to the kitchen and back, then squeezed a long squirt of dish soap on Sébastien's head. But it was too thick. Would it help to add water? The pink roses nodded. I picked up the vase, threw the flowers to my audience, and dumped the water on the little devil's head. *Oh, là là*, I bet all of Paris could hear him now! Most of the people had run up to catch the flowers, but they quickly backed off to avoid getting washed. Then they cheered. Sébastien was free, crying so hard he was drooling. He had soap in his eyes and mouth. The spectators covered their ears and left.

Sylvie clapped. "You're so smart," she said.

Madame Joulié reappeared and yelped, "Sébastien!"

Next, she went into nonstop jabber. She hugged him and checked his head. Then she slapped his behind and peeled the tape off his hair. He howled and howled.

"*Maman*, Véro got him out," said Sylvie.

"Sylvie helped a lot," I said.

"*Merci*, both of you," said her mother.

Just then the doorbell rang.

"Francine," said Sylvie.

Madame Joulié carried a dripping Sébastien to the kitchen and said, "Sylvie, I can't leave him like this. Please answer the door. Good-bye, Véronique."

I kissed Sylvie good-bye, and we left.

What a headache that little Sébastien was! Yet I was glad I'd met him. Borrowing him for an afternoon was great, especially since I could give him back. I was lucky I didn't have a little brother like him. No, Philippe was lucky, because as a little sister, I was nowhere near that much trouble. I hoped he understood that.

Outside Sylvie's apartment building, standing on the sidewalk, hands deep in his pockets, was Philippe. I was speechless. What was he doing there? He led the way and stepped around the soapy splash.

Francine said, "I can't imagine what kind of people would make a mess like this! Not a good girl like you, *mon chou.*" We walked away.

From the open kitchen window upstairs came Madame Joulié's cry, "*Oh, là là,* the bananas!"

But Philippe was busy now, listening to himself talk. "I came to check on how things went—didn't want you to think that I wasn't in charge anymore, you understand. I still have to walk you to and from school, you know. On school days, Francine won't show up until we get home, and she'll leave by dinnertime. Are you going to tell me what you did all afternoon or not? What are you waiting for?"

I told him and Francine how Sylvie and I had saved Sébastien. I had to answer so many questions that it took me all the way home to tell the whole story.

THAT NIGHT, MY PARENTS TOOK US ALL to a nice restaurant. Philippe sat next to me. He and my parents met Francine's husband, and we celebrated their marriage, her return, and how lovely all of our lives had become.